ESCAPE!!!

ESCAPE!!!

J.P. Rodriguez

QUATTRO BOOKS

The publication of ESCAPE!!! has been generously supported by the Canada Council for the Arts and the Ontario Arts Council.

Canada Council for the Arts Conseil des Arts du Canada

ONTARIO ARTS COUNCIL
CONSEIL DES ARTS DE L'ONTARIO
an Ontario government agency
un organisme du gouvernement de l'Ontario

Author photo: Aiden Haw
Editor: Luciano Iacobelli
Cover design and typography: Natasha Shaikh

Library and Archives Canada Cataloguing in Publication

Rodriguez, J. P., author
ESCAPE!!! / J.P. Rodriguez.

ISBN 978-1-927443-84-2 (paperback)

I. Title.

PS8635.O3745E73 2015 C813'.6 C2015-905787-6

Published by Quattro Books Inc.
Toronto
www.quattrobooks.ca

Printed in Canada

For Aiden

A small night storm blows
Saying 'falling is the essence of a flower'
Preceding those who hesitate

—Yukio Mishima

閉

Ground Floor

[on which the passed is never passed enough]

It distinguishes itself from the surrounding scents like a thought bubbling up from the void.

ESCAPE!

!!!

Today of all days. The only day there ever was. He hasn't noticed it in here since her? Has he actually blocked it out? Can a brain do that? Some kind of survival mechanism? Does this noticing it again mean it's safe?

He looks in the mirror and knows exactly who it is. This scent only matches so many. Blond. Natural. Moving aside for the others.

A foreigner.

Gaijin.

外人.

Outside person.

Smiling. As if for him. But it's for everyone. She knows how things work.

Something about her. More than just the perfume.

Reminds him of Sakura.

桜

The nose? The graceful wave of the hair? Her aloneness.

His noticing her?

No.

Must just be the perfume. God how it moves him. Steers him.

And finally, that's what he's going to do.

Escape!

These distinctions and individuations. These boxes.

The *right* way this time.

In the operating-theatre-bright light that masks the late hour but reveals it in their bloodshot eyes and limp hair, the lot of them congregate around the beer fridge and a debate takes place over real beer versus cheap low-malts, then each grabs what they intended to grab in the first place. Will takes two cold cans of premium Yebisu.

"Ooh, high roller," says Sue, Greg's girlfriend, a smooth-skinned trier who never makes any attempt to hide the fact she's interested in Will. She has two small fake beers in her tiny many-ringed fingers.

"Cans of chemicals," says Will of her choice.

"It's *all* chemicals, Will," she returns, then winks. "What do you think your mood's made of? Or your *libido*?"

"But that stuff tastes like garbage."

"It's all shite to me," she says. "Of course you're the expert, yeah? What with your family owning a brewery and all?"

It takes a second for her comment to make sense to him, and in that second the whole night changes—the air gets closer, his jeans get tighter, his voice sticky in his throat, his ability to see good disabled—*But only if I let it*, he reminds himself. "Christ. I wouldn't drink my *dad's* shite if you…" Only if he lets it. "Fucking soulless swill."

She takes a step closer to the till and he makes his legs respond in kind.

"Well, there's no accounting for taste, but you can't argue with price," she says, turning from him to give her beer and money to the love-struck multi-pierced teen standing behind the till obsequiously bowing and smiling like Sue's just told him she wants to sign his band.

Will tries to control his thoughts, resorting to looking at Sue's legs, her white stockings leading up out of yellow Converse and around the bulge of her calves, fabric ending just under her knobby knees, the white of her American thighs leading up under her skirt. He does the math and realises it's been two years since he's been between a pair of these. But life's about control and control's about sacrifice. For a higher purpose, a greater good. He's been making definite progress with his Zen training, but he's well aware there's a forever of hard work ahead of him—which is comforting in a way, meaning as it does that expectations are still low and a wellspring of forgiveness is available to him. And he knows he'll be using up a fair amount of that before he pulls himself out of this ditch of vile mood Sue's thrown him into by mentioning his father.

Back out in the enlightened darkness of the 3AM Shibuya streets he hangs off the back of the giddy pack, drinking his beer in long pulls. The first time he's drunk in he doesn't remember how long, and now proper reason to. His goddamned father. A bloody *brewery* owner? He wishes he'd been a little more creative about that lie, but the irony was too good—the bastard is proud of never having had a drink in his life. As if drinking nothing but bottled water purifies him, absolves him of his sins, his sins of ruining so much and so many, all so he can live up to some fucked-up ideal of power and competence and accomplishment, the élan of the elite; maybe if he'd down a bottle of Jack he'd discover some fucking empathy at the bottom of it!

But Jesus Christ! How many times has he been over this in the last almost-three-years? Thirty-two months now of working and earning his own way, donating every one of his family's ill-gotten dollars that he has access to? A thousand days of training, of trying to defeat his anger and tame his mind, maddest of horses. But everything is training, so he fends off the acidic pique and brings himself back to the humid streets that glow with their own sticky light.

"Can't you guys give it a fucking rest with that damn song!" They're bellowing a drunken Happy Birthday to Ted, yet again. "You sound like a bunch of tacky fucking Yanks!" he yells at them, partly for fun, but mostly for the relief of yelling at someone.

"Hey! It *is* my birthday!" Ted calls back to him.

"Yeah, let him revel! He's likely not got many left!" adds Sue and they all laugh.

"And they love us tacky Yanks here!" tries Alex. "This ain't fookin' France!"

"Shouldn't you be at home meditating anyway!" says Phil, drunkest of them all.

"I'll take him home and give him something to meditate on," says Sue to everyone's idiotic oohs and ahs.

He focuses on his one foot in front of the other, the technique he mastered in the Laurentians, focusing on the earth rotating below him as if he's making it spin, like walking a barrel. But he feels like he's falling off. He thinks of that fall and winter, those nine months he sequestered himself in his family's isolated cottage in Quebec. He'd warned them he'd kill himself if anyone tried to approach, and it was pretty funny, if not scary, how seriously they'd taken him. He'd slept so well in that non-silence, at one with the aloneness, that throbbing vitality of place—the best months of his life. And all made ultimately possible by his family's money, his dad's ridiculously salacious salary defending his corporate clients in the ostensibly-blind-but-actually-eagle-eyed justice system. A couple million a year before bonuses and gifts that amounted to two or three times as much, to manipulate and twist words and meaning and perception and intent and understanding, and, ultimately, reality. Insane. More than insane.

They locate at last a suitable after-hours bar and he trails his friends in, the scent of cigarette smoke, spirits and women's perfume almost overwhelming. Everything that isn't plastic red or painted red or black is red leather, with red lamps everywhere casting the monotony in a cloying light. Heart-shaped stools sit around frosted glass tables and with about ten girls and three guys the place is already halfway to full. With the red and the flesh and the dark corners and the throbbing bass of the electro-pop, he feels like he's stepped into the beating heart of Tokyo. And he feels a sticky sickness rising, a sweaty heaviness.

To his left is a door with 男 on it, the character for "man" (the poor guy bent over with the weight of his family farm on his back (whereas 女, the character for "woman," could signify nothing but sleek and edgy sex)) and so he steps into a red-lighted white-tiled washroom with a big mirror that scares him with a vision of his gaunt glowing-red self. He stands urinating into the polished copper toilet (with mirror-ball flush handle), closes his eyes, feels the throb of the bass and sways to it. The AC vent blows upon him like a winter wind; the stream of his urine feels like it's flowing cold, as if runoff from a glacier melting deep in his stomach—climate change in his *hara?* He zips up and runs the water hot, soaps up his hands and rinses them off, the water so hot it hurts.

Stepping back into the bar he shakes his head as he surveys the scene. Ted, in red, is making the most of it. Ted only ever wears one colour at a time; he says that if everyone did the same a crowd of people would make a much more interesting artistic composition, like pointillist paintings. (Despite Ted being American, Will had thought it such a perfect Asian idea—the masses making the whole, rather than the one making the whole and the masses making a mess.) With a heart-shaped stool under each of his arms and his red hoodie drawn tight around his head so only his big nose and already greying beard sticks out the hole like a wire scrubber, he's posing for photos with all the excited new friends he's about to make. Of course non-Asian *outside* people will always get a good response from a crowd—just another tricky dimension of the way Japanese treat Western foreigners: on an altar, yes, but also of a different species. He notices that even the DJ is laughing at Ted's antics.

And then he *really* notices the DJ, headphones hugging long silky hair that hangs straight down either side of her shoulders, a river of black ink bifurcating into two streams round a headland, proposing the impossible task of choosing front or back, a gentle wave pattern to the flow as she moves to her music. She stands in the only white light in the room. He's completely outside himself, drawn by an instant attachment he's defenceless against—after a thousand days of training! But at least all thoughts of his father have now been rendered as attention-worthy as Styrofoam packing. He steps up to her table and falls into her black hole eyes. In Japanese he says, "Have you got *Slow Hands*?"

Her pencil thin lips curl into a knowing smile. "Which remix?" she replies, also in Japanese, her tone asking him if he really thinks he can win so easily.

2nd Floor

[on which bubbles are burst]

"Everyone inside? Oop, mind your bag, Ma'am. There you go. Thank you. Doors closing."

Reeling from the ESCAPE.

Ok. Fine. Good. But still …

!

In control again, he slides the index finger of his white-gloved hand off the open button, carves a little loop and lands it on the button for close, 閉, the character like a man with his head smashed between two gates. Two worlds. The gone and the coming.

Him.

But then there's the button for open, 開, like the man's head's gone now, like he's free of it, he's escaped it, all the madness in there. He's all feel now, all gut, *hara*, strong shoulders, present. Only in the moment.

Him soon.

How he wishes he had a second. Avoid the burn. No. It's what will cleanse. The capital in the Art.

Shaking.

He desperately wants to look at her reflection again, but resists.

"Welcome to Ikiruji Center. We are honoured to have you. This elevator will stop at the second floor next, where you will find various …" he drones on and on, automatically, his voice superfluous and sterile, white-gloved above the hum and the whir.

"We have now arrived, valued customers, at floor fifteen. Please mind the doors opening now." He looks at his watch. "Enjoy yourselves please. Many fine foods and drinks." Fifty-five minutes till he's done. "Mind your step." … Some leave. … Some come. He closes the door and spills his spiel and thinks of her again. Their three hours last night. Three hours unlike any three hours he's experienced in … he doesn't really remember any three hours like it, perhaps not since grade 8, and Wendy, tripping over sidewalks in a daze of her, writing her name endlessly and drawing her face on school notebooks. It feels like being brought down to bare essence. His mind reminds him that did not end well, but then reminds him that nothing ultimately does and so what the hell exactly are you supposed to do in the meantime. He's filled with a desire and the accompanying energy to seize the world, to lean into it full-on, to try to arrest its advance and see what it will do.

Sakura—*Cherry Blossoms*, 桜—as Japanese as you get. Studying international law at nowhere less than *Tokyo* University. The unapologetic product of her politician parents. The course of her life charted before she'd exited the womb—"Before even entering it, actually," she said, but with no discernable hint of regret or whimsy. In fact, she seemed happy about it—content, perhaps, having a place and knowing it? Or maybe it was about balance—given such a *yin*, she could feel justified taking this term off, indulging in a *yang* of bohemian thrill-seeking, part of which includes DJ-ing at the bar her parents had bought for her brother so he'd appear successful. And part of which is going to include him?

But even this is more than he wants to know about her; if there's anything he knows, it's that the less you know about a person the easier it is to make them who you need them to be.

For the 797th time today he asks himself what the hell he's going to do. Is he going to call her? Is he going to call her? Text? Is he going to risk everything? Is he going to call her? Is he going to deny himself this too? In the absence, the impossibility, of certainty, should not the heart win out?

Ridiculous thought! Isn't that how humans have created this mess we're in? Is he going to call her? Fuck!

16th floor. All rush out. And … *none* come in?

?

He pops his head around and looks.

!

桜!

!

Saying something to the couple standing beside her.

!

Now she's bowing repeatedly as she backs away from them and into the elevator.

!

In his box. With him. Just her. And him. And her perfume. "Escape," she said. Perfect.

He presses 閉.

But feels more like 開.

"Going up?" she says with a knowing mischievous smile.

The doors close and they're alone. "Can't go higher than this," he tells her, and presses 15, vaguely remembering he told her he worked here and she'd been intrigued.

"So, this is your office," she jokes. "Could do with some windows," she continues, reaching over to push his buttons—specifically 止, and the elevator comes to a jarring halt. "The world could do with an emergency stop button, don't you think?"

"I ..." he says, stupidly.

"What time are you finished?" Her eyes are fearless, as though she knows well what fear is but nothing rules her—the very state he's been fighting so long to achieve.

"Six."

"Meet me at Dutour?"

"Of course."

Her gaze is hard on him now, eyes focusing like telescopes, taking in light from light years inside him. Now she smiles; maybe she's found the exploding star she was looking for?

She reaches and releases the emergency stop and the elevator continues on its now throbbing way. His heart's racing, as if the elevator's moving from his own exertion. The doors open and she exits without another word, like a thief fleeing the sight of the theft. He wants to just walk out with her, leave his box forever, but people are piling in and she's out of sight.

But why not look?

His last day in this shit show; make the most of it and do this right.

Why on earth did he come in to work today?

How has he even managed to remain on his feet?

He looks at her again. Blond hair. Looking at her feet.

Because it felt necessary.

He can't believe it.

Is this proving him right?

ESCAPE!

They don't even make it anymore, Sakura said.

This girl. How come today? *This* day?

Sakura. In *Gaijin* form. Come to tempt him again? Come to rub his nose in it?

Where is she now?

He never even knew her.

He'd impressed himself upon her, telling himself that if he could lose himself in her he could forget about everything wrong and getting worse in this woeful world, that losing himself in passion would be easier and more effective than losing his self in Zen discipline. And to assuage the lashings of guilt, he'd told himself he could be wrong about the wrong in the world; he could be wrong about the wrongness of being with her.

He hadn't even known the half of it.

Not that he does now either.

But he has no interest in it any longer.

Above and beyond it.

6:08 and time has an air of impossibility about it that's exaggerated by the pattern of scratched tile floor, the smell of coffee and leather, the too-bright of the lights, the crowd and the amalgam of voices. *Her, near the back.* Green highlighter in hand, she's busy reading an old hardcover with no dust jacket, and as she hears the poof of the leather as he drops into the chair across from her she looks up and smiles. She's wearing glasses and her eyes seem wizened behind them, as if they're not there to help her see others more clearly, but for the likes of riffraff like him to see her properly.

"Thanks for coming," she says, a boss thanking her staff for attending a mandatory meeting; a boss adored by her employees.

"It was easy. I get to use the company elevator."

She smiles, as if she thinks the dumb joke deserved it. "Did you get in trouble then?"

He searches his brain for a clue to what she's talking about, and thankfully it comes through for him somewhat. "No. No …"

"That's good. Wouldn't want to be responsible for you losing your job." That bend in her lips again.

"Oh, no worries about that," he says, trying to decide whether what's his to lose is nothing or everything. He catches again her glorious scent, which invades his very being like daylight pouring through a wall that's been torn down.

"Ever been stuck in there?"

"Yes," he answers, which is true.

She settles deeper into her chair, stopping time. "Really?"

"Well sure. You know the numbers."

"What numbers?"

"Elevators are notoriously unreliable. They've got a breakdown rate of, like, point zero zero zero two percent. So one in fifty-thousand rides will fail."

"One in fifty-thousand?"

"Which doesn't sound like much, I know, but imagine planes failing at that rate. It'd be a plane a day."

Now she looks sceptical, her eyes narrow, a rising sun peeking through a gap where the ceiling of cloud doesn't quite reach the horizon. What could be more compelling, more worth looking at?

"We have to train, you know? It's not just pushing buttons. Even had to write a test." She's shaking her head, her sharp lips slightly parted, readying to question. "We have to be good. People die. They walk through doors that open with no elevator there and fall into the shaft, or their scarf gets caught and they get strangled." She's looking for a toehold as he hears himself carrying on, "In nineteen-forty-five a bomber in the fog crashed into the Empire State Building and the elevator free-fell seventy-five floors, but the operator didn't die."

"Because he was good?"

"Because *she* knew that shaft so well she knew exactly when impact was going to come and she jumped."

She stares at him a moment, then laughs, beautifully.

He smiles. "She did survive, though. It's a Guinness record. I read it on Wikipedia."

She sips her tea, looks him up and down. "What were some of the questions on the test?"

"Lots of mechanical stuff, physics and first aid and whatnot, some essay questions."

"*Essay* questions?"

He wonders where the hell he's going with all this, but his neurons are dancing, the effervescence of a mosh pit. In a *good* way. "Sure. Like, explain the impact elevators have had on the development of the modern city and the further impact on the modern psyche."

There's a real fun-loving glint in her eye now, so intoxicating. "And your answer?"

"While allowing cities to rise higher and grow denser, they have also resulted in compartmentalization of the mind, and isolation, discomfort with closeness, dislocation and local distance, hyper focus on one's space and therefore one's separation and distinction from others. The most intimate us and them. We get closer, but farther apart. But no more us and them, actually, just me and you all. A bubble universe."

She looks at him quizzically, as if she's now not sure whether or not he's being serious. This is Japan after all. And she's Japanese. Though far from typical—has he heard of anyone taking a semester off here?

"Another was about the ethics of dating clients." Whoa! "I expounded upon fairness in love and war."

She leans her head to one side, resting it on the knuckles of her right hand and squinting at him, sunrise eyes again.

"Okay, okay. Joking."

"*Thank* you."

"But mine *did* get stuck once. For twenty minutes. A five-year-old really had to pee so he did and we all had to stand in it. When we made it to the next floor, mall staff were waiting with a pair of slippers for everyone and they took the shoes to a cleaner and took everyone to the shoe store where they were allowed to pick any pair of shoes they wanted for free." At least that story's true. Sort of—the boy had actually peed into a water bottle someone emptied by drinking the water.

"Must've stunk," she says, glancing over to the young teenage couple beside them who keep looking over at them, no doubt caught up in her beauty, and him, an *outside person,* speaking insider's Japanese.

"They let them keep the slippers as well," he adds.

She sharpens her gaze on him once again, and he senses she wants more, she wants deeper; she wants in. Or maybe she just can't believe how ridiculous he is, because he's certainly feeling that all of a sudden. "So," she says, "is this the entry position in some grand plan to rise through the ranks of the elevator pilots to someday become, what? Sergeant? General? Is there a *Kamikaze* squad?"

!

Kamikaze.

神風.

Divine wind.

"The sixteenth floor is as high as I'm going to rise with this job. And I reached that on my first ride so …"

"How about Toranomon Hills? Or the Skytree? Burj Khalifa someday. You have no dreams?"

"None that I remember upon waking." He didn't even mean it to be anything more than cynical, but she's taken more from it. She seems to be weighing him now, out of his uniform, out of the fluorescent light of the mall, element for element. He has the distinct impression that she's judging his suitability, his worthiness, for something. Something big he hopes. A divine wind?

"What are you doing here, Will? One of the last elevator drivers in Japan. You obviously could be doing a lot more with your looks and your language ability. You could be on TV."

"Trapped in an even smaller box. One I have no control over?"

She gives a little squint and then her right eyebrow is dragged up by her furrowed brow, a provocation delivered with the mastery of an actress. He's always wished he could do that. Intrigued and beguiled, he wants to see something that might give him a clue as to what this girl is and isn't about. She's unreadable. There's nothing fake or forced or unnatural about her, even her makeup seems to have simply fallen on. And yet she seems supremely in control of herself, as though nothing affects her, as though she's a prime mover.

"I teach English part time, too. A little conversation school in Ooimachi that—"

"All I want when I'm in an elevator," she says over his *Ooimachi that*, "is out."

How many different ways to interpret that? He wonders again how much to give away. All? Nothing? "I do it … to see if I can handle it … I used to like the looks I'd get from people, seeing a *gaijin* doing this job."

"You like standing out?"

"I like forcing myself to ignore it … try to make it real instead of practice."

"And forcing others to do the same?" she says.

Not bad. "Kinda sorta maybe."

She opens her mouth to say something, seems to reconsider, then says, "How long have you been doing it? Not exactly a resume builder."

"Six months now. It helps me train."

A spark in her eyes. "For what? Standing competitions?"

"Well, for one thing, I'm claustrophobic."

She's deciding whether or not to believe him and he suddenly wants nothing more than to have her believe forever and always everything he ever says.

"A claustrophobic *elevator* driver?"

"Well, I was. Mental control … I'm something of a …" All the words he can think of sound idiotic, and he realizes he hasn't spoken to anyone like this in years. *Years.* Well, other than *her, last night.* So he chooses to believe that the look in her eye says she likes what she's hearing. That he's not going to come off as just another gawky white Westerner infatuated with all things Japan and believing *he's* the one who *really* gets it. "Let's just say I believe a lot of our problems stem from the fact that we've got these big fancy brains in our heads but we just let them do whatever they want. We're just along for the ride, you know? Which, in a world wallowing in physical and mental pollution, is a pretty big problem."

"Like, being in an elevator with a driver who pushes the buttons for us?"

He smiles and can't imagine himself ever tiring of the minute movements and transitions her face goes through as she listens to him.

She finishes the remainder of her coffee, tucks her black bangs behind her perfectly formed ear, and then, as she looks into her empty cup, her bangs fall alluringly back over her face. She does not replace them when she looks back at him. She's now a samurai sizing up a new sword. "How did you acquire such good Japanese?"

She asked him this last night, and he wonders if she's not testing him, for consistency of answers. "I studied hard. I love the *kanji.* Guess I have a head for it as well."

She considers, as if trying to decide if she can believe anything he has to say. "Speaking of your head," she says, "it's shaved for the summer heat, or is it your mind-control business? You a Buddha, Will?"

"It's nothing religious. Not capital R, anyway."

Just then the couple next to them gets up to leave and one of the girl's many slick shopping bags hits Sakura's cup and rattles it. The girl blushes and makes multiple deep bows and excuse-mes and then they're walking away behind Will's back. Sakura's watching them, an impenetrable expression on her face, in her eye a wisp of about five hairs that he wants to reach out and clear away for her.

"Sometimes I think I'd like to burn down this mall," she says suddenly, her tone unknowable, as if she's simply trying out the words, seeing how they work together, the feeling behind it either perfectly complete or perfectly absent. Her eyes are back on him, watching, as if to see if she can make out any movement under his shaved skull. Knocking on the glass of a fishbowl.

"Are you serious?"

"You want me to be?"

He's stuck, no words, dangerous ground.

She laughs. "Well, Will," she says, "better get on home."

An entire quiver of arrows through his hot air balloon. "What station are you?"

"Twenty-minute walk from here."

"I'll walk you."

His parachute opens as she puts up no resistance, and he's floating through the warm sky down and out into the dayglo night streets of Shinjuku, which are crowded as ever and hot and humid and all sultry closeness, fitting but unusual this early in the year. He walks with her down progressively narrower and emptier and darker streets to the door of a house in an old neighbourhood he never would have guessed existed. "I'm the main floor," she says, offering no further explanation.

"I never imagined Shinjuku was a local station for anyone. The absolute heart of Tokyo."

"For me and my neighbours it is."

"A *neighbourhood.*"

"How long have you been here? Turn a corner in Japan and you never know what you're going to find there."

"Full of surprises."

"Maybe I'll come take a spin or two on your ride tomorrow."

Another perfect demonstration. What is this? Can it be trusted?

"Unless when I Google you I find out you're wanted or something."

Damn. Again, all or nothing to lose? "In that case, I guess you better hear it from me."

"What?" The deepest interest her face has shown yet. And the most satisfying beauty.

"Four years ago … I dumped, well, a barrel of oil onto the financial district in Toronto."

"What?"

"Well, a half barrel's worth."

"You're kidding."

"Performance art, sort of. And I spent some time in jail."

"You went to *jail*?"

"Sixty days. Discovered my claustrophobia there. I admit it *was* naïve, but …"

"And now you're the last elevator driver in a Tokyo department store."

"I'm kind of, in a holding pattern, I suppose."

"… like a broken elevator."

"Not broken. Just closed for training."

"I was only joking about blowing up the mall, you know?" She says it with what appears to be mock concern. Again the sense that she's making this up as she goes along. That she's in some sort of game show where she has to convince some sucker that she's intrigued by him.

What?

"Really?"

"Well …" She winks, says bye, then turns to open the door.

He turns away and starts up the street, trying to hold his head together.

"Hey," he hears, "hold on."

He turns and waits in the warm still air. Ten seconds later she comes back to him and takes his hand, turns his wrist up, sprays some ESCAPE there, smiles, and then disappears into her house.

His train, the Chuo, 中, central, through the middle of Tokyo, a samurai slice cleaving one in two, cell division, procreation, symmetry and equality, a fair division, a perfect pairing, balance and divine grace, comes, and he gets on.

Behind him the doors 閉.

It's crowded. Lots of smells. ESCAPE strongest as he holds onto the bar above him and rests his face against his forearm.

Nice to be in a box he's not driving, nothing he has to say. One that's going somewhere.

In a bubble universe, they're all all to themselves.

His station.

Open doors.

開.

3rd Floor

[on which the elevator can no longer contain him]

The elevator sheds a few people and gains a few more and she's staying with him. How high is she going?

"Welcome, dear customers. Please, step in, step in. Welcome."

ESCAPE.

Escape.

And Sakura.

Properly invading his brain now.

"Welcome dear customers."

No! This is *not* about her!

But this perfume drags him right back into the thick of it, the thick of her hair, the thick wet heat of their togetherness. Their two months. Of not love, but a dream life, escape from frustration and anger and responsibility, caring for nothing beyond here-and-now-and-me-in-it.

"Please mind, doors closing now. And now dear customers, welcome to this physics-defying leap from the third to the *fifth* floor."

Whoa, new wording. What's his brain doing?

"A journey through space and time, *woorumuhoruzu* and dimensions." Ridiculous.

Ah Sakura … How could you be so stupid?

Back in his tiny corner of the world he opens the windows on either side of his desk, feels the humid air pressing in, sweating as if alive and working hard at something. He sips his beer and looks out at the planted fields surrounding the building, the plot edged by houses, apartments and the road, the opposite of Shinjuku. Shinjuku of today anyway. 新宿, which means new station, or post town, where those travelling across the country would stay for the night. Not *live*. Is she real? Is any of this real?

Shinjuku. The electric strobing lascivious non-stop beep and clatter and calling of Japan's heart, with Sakura in it, of it.

Shinjuku, the heart of a city that was 90 percent destroyed in the war. Destroyed by us. *Us,* so welcome now. Not only forgiven, but elevated? But is it true? Have they really let any of us in? Or do they laugh at our pride, our egoism, our grandeur, our lack of subtlety and refinement? Our clumsy lack of art and grace. Our convinced self-love. Is she just playing with him? Using him? Is that what they all do with us? Or are they themselves caught, consumed in the contagion of our ostentation?

Jesus, is his mind firing off! Jesus, is he paranoid? He laughs and downs the rest of his beer and into the second begins to feel the familiar raising and narrowing. This beer, the first he's drank in almost half a year—other than last night—is purely celebratory; he'd fight it off if that felt like the right thing to do, but it doesn't. And it feels more right by sip and by second. He wants to paint. Nothing more than to paint. The essence of him rearing up under the influence. But he has no canvas. He has his sketchpad, but he needs to paint large, life-size. He needs to paint her. Literally *her*?

He cracks a third can and swallows till it burns, then goes to the closet and pulls out his acrylics. He feels alive and he feels good. Innervated and vigorous. Ready to be as he looks around him. Four walls, a ceiling and a floor. The room's a box. Like the elevator, another box, but one that can't move him.

The south wall contains the door, the west the dresser and a big window matching another on the north wall, his desk wedged into the corner they form. The last wall, shared with the neighbour, has his single bed pressed up against it and the closet at the foot of it. He sits and listens to the shades of silence. He can swear he hears cicadas, but it's too shallow in the year to hear the calls of those insects with the most depressing of lives. He puts his headphones in his ears and selects Nootropics, finishes off the half beer and opens the last. He spins around in his chair and comes to rest facing his bed and the windowless wall. And an idea blooms in him. This room *can* move him.

Eight hours later the train rolls to a stop at 新宿 and he alights, revelling in the past-rush-hour-less-than-insanely-busyness of the station, makes his way out the east exit and retraces his steps from the previous evening to her door. The fact that it worked seems somehow unbelievable to him, as likely as rewinding time itself. He's not nervous as he rings the bell, for he's already told himself that if she isn't there it's because she's at Ikiruji trying to find him to make him leave sick and spend the day at the park with her under the cherry blossoms—桜—which will soon begin falling from the trees. But she's there, an enigmatic smile on her face as she sees it's him; the smile that seems like a conversation with itself. And that's fine, because he's determined to limit this.

"Elevator down? They don't need you today?" she says somewhat demurely, as if embarrassed for not calling what it is what it is. This surprises him.

"They don't need me at work any day. It's an experiment in meaninglessness." The words feel like a promise he's making. But it's not the promise he wants to make anymore. She'll understand. He'll make her. What is he saying? Who is it saying this? He's trying. Keep this shallow and utilitarian, like a beach holiday to an uninteresting country.

She doesn't say anything at first, as if wanting him to go on, but he's said enough already. "Want to come in?"

"Doesn't matter. You can come out."

"Give me a minute."

He sits on the curb and stares across the road and into the little concrete-walled box of a park where the trees are busying themselves with blooming their coat of green for the impending summer. There are no cherry trees in there. As he waits, he finds himself craving a cigarette. Something, anything, to do. He sits on the curb, makes his back erect and tries meditating, tries to pound his mind into submission:

… God, she's*POUND*
… What are you even*POUND*
… You know she*POUND*

... Wonder what she*POUND*
... Imagine what herP*OUND*
... How *do* you make a bomb*POUND*

And then, thank God and Buddha and Allah and Zeus, she's at his side. He tries not to size her up. Only notices that she's wearing neat black Vans slip-ons and little tiny black socks that allow all the world to witness the smooth white flesh that covers the bones of her beautiful slender ankles that lead up to a definite rounding of runner's calves and narrow again to the perfectly formed diamonds of her knees which widen out to thighs that make their way under her pleated grey skirt which itself narrows to her waist which is hidden just under the slightly loose-fitting Matisse-green t-shirt that—

"What are you thinking?"

"Ummm, well ..." Why is it that a woman can turn the most trained and dedicated mind to—

"Let's go to Shinjuku Park. Count the blossoms that fall."

"Sounds perfect."

They set to walking and he gets himself together, until she takes him by the hand and he catches the scent of her ESCAPE.

"So, I did look you up last night."

Aha! "And."

"No comment."

"Not a one?"

"None. Definitely not a one."

"Well, myself, I was all set to look up bomb-making, but then I realized it wouldn't be too long before the SDF were breaking down my door to extradite me to Guantanamo."

"Only after torturing you for answers first, I'd imagine."

"But they'd get nothing from me, I swear."

"You are a Buddha."

She meant it jokingly, but he feels an oddly strong need to set her straight on that. "I don't mind you joking about it, but I do want you to know what you're dealing with here." Maybe some frivolous and futile need to be properly understood, maybe stemming from some silly issue he's got from being so misunderstood by his parents, some silly shit like that. God he hates shit like that.

She stops and faces him, takes his other hand in her own and looks up to him. "Then tell me. What am I dealing with here?"

He thinks about that, reminding himself of that sage advice to be careful what you ask for. "I meditate, but it's just like working out your body to gain more control over it and make it able to do things better. Like training a dog. Nothing to do with a god."

Her eyes survey his chin, his cheeks, his forehead, and then fall back to his eyes. She smiles. "You look a bit like Mishima, you know?"

Mishima! The man-of-integrity's man-of-integrity! "Mishima. As in Yukio?"

"Exactly as in, yes."

"He's my favourite Japanese writer."

"Eh. My dad says I should steer clear of him. Says he was a psychopath."

"He may have been a bit crazy, but the last thing he was is a psychopath." Careful with the defensiveness.

"But something sexy about him." She's looking at him hard, knowingly insulting and defiant, restlessly prurient, a giant stick in the spokes of his mind. "Something in your eyes. And your brows."

"Hopefully it's not my neck," he manages, and she laughs. "Probably just my shaved head."

"Perhaps," she says, and then lets go of his right hand, continuing him along the road and all the way to the entrance of the park, walking so quickly, even skipping like a child at times. He's again taken by how the world and its workings can be so bleak and yet one little thing can make it all suddenly seem worthwhile, necessary even. *Good*, even. David and forty-seven Goliaths. And this girl seems part of that paradox—a depth of awareness and discontent seems clear in her restless eyes and slightly too-tall forehead, and it's obvious that she's weighed down by what she knows, yet she's strong enough to skip along despite it—and makes him want to do the same.

Art is about moving us toward ecstasy.

They pay the entrance fee and head into the depths where the trees are in full bloom and the park's loaded with people, 人々—literally person doubled up—making the most of the beauty, a beauty that's short-lived and thus all the more intense, like the sun in winter. It's crowded but nothing like the weekend when people come the night before to stake a claim for their tarp and then sleep on it. And then, when Saturday or Sunday comes it will be wall-to-wall—tree-to-tree—a quilt of distinct cells that will bleed into one another as the day wears on and more alcohol is consumed. Nothing but jubilation and convincing revelry.

She takes hold of him and pulls him out to the middle of an open expanse of grass dotted with groups of people but plenty of spaces between, upon one of which they sit. She presses her skirt into her lap and sits cross-legged. He tries not to stare.

She leans back on her palms, as if to demonstrate being pulled away from him. Her control over her attraction? Her power? Her eyes remain on him. She seems to be weighing up truths. As if in warning, the wail of a fire engine slashes its way into the air, so proud of itself, then abruptly cuts to silence. An emergency nearby. She *laughs* at it and looks hard at him, that evaluating summarizing gaze, as if she refuses to let her gut rule her.

He's fighting his tongue, so much he wants but doesn't want to give of himself, to unload; he's desperate for her to speak first, but she's beaten him to the fifth. She inhales deeply and he sees she's a stage actor. Out of necessity. Or maybe desire. Or maybe just sheer fuckery. Or is this the real her now. She's come out, tentative, baring virgin skin to the direct rays of the sun. Daring it. But scared of getting burnt? Now she's looking at the tarp nearest them, a group of nine twenty-somethings laughing and lurching and prodding and drinking in circular formation around a nucleus of cans of beer and bottles of *sochu* and plastic trays of food as if they're performing a ceremony to it. She looks back to him and he wants her to again tell him she wants to burn down the mall, but she doesn't, just maintains her silence, as if waiting for him to remember his lines and believing she won't be helping him if she tells him the answer.

"Are you thirsty?" is what leaks through his vocal chords to dribble through his lips.

She could spit in his face, she could get up and walk away, she could do a half-backflip and break her neck, but she does none of those or the zillion other things she might, that would never measure up to what she does; she leans into him and kisses him, probing her tongue into his mouth and his own tongue engages of its own will. And it isn't until she pulls away from him that he realizes his mind's gone gorgeously blank. The scent of her ESCAPE lingers with that of the cherry blossoms, in beautiful harmony.

She whispers something but it gets eaten up by a sudden thrust of wind that lifts skirts and edges of tarps and sends plastic wrappings and blossom petals madly swirling through the air. A couple of children run by, the one in the lead clearly faster but trying to keep it sporting.

He's afraid to give his vocal chords even an inch, but he senses frustration in her now, as if she's cast into a teeming river three times and come up empty. And yet here he's bought—hook line sinker rod and tackle box—everything she's offering!

He takes her left hand and holds it, notes its sharp delicacy, a *kanji* character tattooed on her narrow wrist, elaborate and stylized; he feels like he knows it, but his brain is turned upside down and inside out, no help at all. 侍. He'd take ten years off the end of his life to be granted the ability to read this back to her. To prove something to her. "Sorry Sakura, I'm coming up blank," he says and the sound of his voice fills him with the oddest sensation, like stage fright, like she's Schrödinger's cat and any words he says will be tantamount to opening the box, ending her superposition of respecting him and thinking him a fool, forcing her to one or the other, one he fears he can not live with, one which will end his own superposition of being alive and dead at the same time. It's absurd and he almost laughs, but it's like his life's at stake. No, he feels like the *meaning* of his life is at stake. He's a *Kamikaze* in his Zero, diving at the target—hit it and live, miss it and die. His logic had been so sound before. His intent so pure. What's this? There's about this girl a resonant sense of impossible possibility that seems to distort and throw into question every single thing he's previously known and felt.

He looks at her wrist again, and there it is! Could it be? She steers clear of Mishima, but she has this tattoo? He fearlessly breaks his silence, cats be damned. "It's samurai."

She smiles a smile he swears is that of someone who's just caught sight of an oasis in a desert, but that's so over the top he wonders if he's just imagining it. Imagining all of this. And the smile in him overpowers hers; could it be she's just as thirsty as everyone else?

5th Floor

[on which prison is explained]

She's still with him. Not wanting to get off on the death floor.

It's called five, but she knows.

Floor 4, avoided in the East like 13 in the West.

Ridiculousness.

Except, they have something of a logical reason for it, as *four* is pronounced *shi*, which is a synonym for death.

One, two, three, *death*, five, six, seven, eight.

Death.

死.

Which, fittingly, leaves as much room for creativity as any *kanji* he's ever considered, given that the constituent radicals are:

一 which means one.

匕 which means spoon

夕 which means evening

He imagines a button with death on it.

He imagines pressing it. If that was all it took. For some it is.

He shakes his head and stands up straighter.

Announces that 6 will be next.

By 6:00 they're in the lounge on the thirty-fourth floor of the Shinagawa Prince hotel, in a semicircular booth of their own in front of a wall of windows facing west as the sun drops way out there in the haze.

"Incredible when you can look at the sun like this," she says, "its edges as sharp as the moon. Like truth suddenly coming into focus."

"Impossible to believe it's fire."

"But it'll burn you."

"Ninety-nine percent of the solar system's mass."

She looks at him. "Seriously? … We're mostly fire?"

"Some of us more than others," he says, smiling.

Their drinks arrive, vodka, cassis and soda with lemon—Sakura's recommendation—and he takes a sip. "Mmm," he says.

They sit silent and looking; when the sight of the largest built-up area in the world is laid out before you, it can be difficult to think of what to say, never even mind the Sakura effect. The sun's about to be cut down by the serrated edge of the distant mountains that bound the Kanto plain, which is actually a sea, a still cubist sea of concrete, glass and steel, chaotic blocky waves of disjointed dimension and sentiment, fitful flows of cars weaving their ever-interrupted way through the interstices, and people unseen but crammed in everywhere. Everywhere. People. 人々. Dense strata of them housed in all these boxes. But at this divine but brief time of year, the blooming of the cherry blossoms, there are bursts of white pink everywhere, as if some sane painter has taken a monumentally realistic painting of a cityscape and dabbed impressionistic splotches of paint all over it.

"Don't you ever get sick of the city?" Sakura says, the last rays of the sun pouring into her eyes, giving them a fourth dimension. She does not squint.

"Can't imagine who wouldn't," he says, aiming for more.

She takes a sip of her drink, leaving a stain of red on the white plastic. He wonders how many more of his answers will disappoint her. He ups the ante. "I spent eight months completely away from people once."

Now she looks interested again; in such contrast is this face to the last he feels that if all he does for the rest of his life is keep this look there, he'll be doing the greatest possible good that he can for the world. Yet, a feeling of … what's with this need to please?

"Eight months? Where when why? How?"

Now that he's backed himself into explaining it, he feels weary. But what the hell, they're only words. "After I got out of jail, I had to get away, I didn't want to just be *travelling* … so I rented a car and drove north and ended up in this smallish town, Thunder Bay, such a cool name and suitably North American dive-ish for a town, but authentic, textured, in the middle of nowhere, train tracks and grain elevators and scruffy strips, rednecks and out of control beards, bar fights strip clubs potholes pickups, beating up fags and spitting on Indians, but also art galleries and nice restaurants and poetry readings and fair-trade stores and blues festivals and Pow Wows and serious sailing, all stuck between an endless sea of trees and the biggest lake in the world. I rented the top floor of a big old house with a view of the lake and this gorgeous mountain shaped like a giant sleeping on his back out at the head of the bay, and I just existed there. Painting every day, reading, daylong walks, a moment-by-moment basic existence to figure out what the hell the point of my life was going to be. I lived off my parents' money, telling myself they owed it to me, that I was putting it to good use trying to shape myself into someone other than them. Well, my dad didn't know about the money, just my mother. Till it hit me that all I was really doing was what I wanted when I wanted, exactly what they and everyone like them do. So I got a job at McDonald's. And I got a room at a cheap motel called Lakeview that had no view and no lake, but now …"

"You were Cocker's Common People girl."

"Jesus, Sakura! Exactly. *Exactly.* I'd actually sing that song to myself so I could say I got the irony and therefore it wasn't me. But it was. *But still you'll never get it right, cuz when you're laying in bed at night, watching roaches climb the wall, if you called your dad he could stop it all, yeah!* … Sorry, I'm going long here, aren't I?"

"It's fascinating. Just let me go to the bathroom. You order us a couple more of these."

With that she's gone, leaving him locked in the incriminating lyrics of the Pulp tune. *Fascinating.* He orders the drinks then turns his gaze out the window. The sun's set completely now but the sky glows, betraying its presence still, but offering no proof it'll ever decide to come back. Like the lingering scent of ESCAPE on his clothing.

But Sakura does come back, her presence made stronger by her absence. She's touched up her makeup and her red lips stand in perfectly firm contrast to the black of her hair, her long lashes calling out dangerously, the thorns of a rose.

The drinks come and he watches her lips tighten and clench around another straw, then separate as she gently releases it and settles back into the bench, her hair falling gracefully across her face on the left side, hanging straight down on the right but lifting into the subtlest trace of a wave at the end. He feels alive, the master and conductor of every proton and electron of his body, except for his blood, surging, his heart light, as though the blood's alive and pumping itself and his heart's only there to make sure it doesn't get out of control and burst right out of him.

"Tell me the rest of it," she says.

He swims through the haze of her and back into his past, pulling at the anchor of his history, which feels so heavy yet so empty in the retelling. Maybe he can make it right. "So I needed to get a feel for just how lucky I really was. It makes my blood boil to hear damn American politicians rave on about how they're the greatest country in the world, how Westerners are so rich because we're so talented and industrious and hardworking, as if everyone else in the world are lazy weak stupid bumbling fools who can scarcely avoid tripping every third step."

She laughs, and looks as surprised as he is by it. "Sorry, that's just a funny image."

"So, I went to India, Calcutta and Varanasi, then Nepal, and I hated it. I looked at these locals getting by on, like, ten cents a day, saw me and the other Westerners blowing a hundred, a thousand times that, a fucking *million* times that, and I thought about how my family's money, just my one nuclear family, could … Anyway, I fell into a bit of Buddhism like everyone does, and it made me feel a real need to get away from other humans, and then the tsunami hit, the arm of mother nature just wiping us, well, *them,* away, like sweat from her brow, and I couldn't stop thinking about it, all the images and video of panic horror struggle loss. I kind of got addicted to it, my eyes desperate for it, hours and hours, Youtubing myself down the drain, trying to get inside of it, to feel it all at once, to *understand* it. I thought I might go crazy, and maybe I did a little. I truly did not trust myself, what I might do." He stops there, not wanting to go down that track, and surprised by the lack of shock on her face; suddenly he feels like a novelty act, a curiosity, a child acting cute?

"So you tried to walk away from it all?"

"Yeah, well, not quite, I …" He thinks of how to explain, how not to make a mistake, how to *sell it?* But he knows he can't, so he tries to just get it over with. "I decided I wasn't going to care anymore, that one minute you're sitting on the beach, the next you're buried below it and the only thing to regret is wasted opportunity. *Of all the words of mice and men, the saddest are, it might have been.* So, I did six-months of heady head-on hedonism, steeped in nihilism and self-pity and reckless abandon, blowing my mind and my parents' money with any friend it could make, telling my parents I was just going to travel a little longer and then I *would* start my MBA and …" He feels ridiculous. It was ridiculous. It fucking *is* ridiculous. "Until I was in Borders one day, in Manhattan, unhappy and hung over as hell and feeling massively unmanly, cancerous, and I ended up picking up *The Pillars of Zen*. You know it?"

"No."

"Well, I'd not really read much on Zen before, but this was so down my street. I realized right then and there, right on 7th Avenue, that I had to get away from everything that was poisoning me before I became terminal. So I took that book and a bunch of others and I took off to our Quebec cottage and I stayed there eight months, only ever talking to the guy who delivered my orders. It wasn't Walden, it was luxury, but all I needed was to get away in every way from people. To get *me* out of my mind. And it kind of worked. And then I came here. And I … Holy fuck, how much can one person talk about himself?" He feels silly for that last sentence—is he not willing to be perfectly honest with her? Does he not have faith in the stoutness of his foundation? He dives for his drink and most of the ice has melted so he drinks it down in one go.

She smiles, but it falls away. "And so what now?"

"I'm still working on that. Still searching, I guess. Still mostly working on training myself."

"That could take thousands of incarnations. You think you've got enough time?"

"Inspiration doesn't grow on trees."

"You're the first white guy I've ever kissed."

"Be prepared for the sixth floor, our next stop, dearly valued shoppers and spenders of great dollars."

This ESCAPE and an *outside person*, 外人, feels so wrong. So not right.

Throws him.

Worlds colliding. Disparate dimensions folding in on themselves and leaving scientists scratching their heads.

He looks down and toes his box more perfectly into the corner.

Another box containing him.

He rests his foot on it, but it's too flimsy and the side collapses a bit.

"Floor six. There you will find many fine items for home cleaning and beautification. Please, honourable customers, be prepared to alight here for all your—."

Fuck, the knife is slipping …

"—home lifestyle needs."

… out of position.

An elevator driver with a knife falling out of his pants. A foreign one. Not acceptable. Particularly in this age of terror and who knows who out to kill you. Even his whiteness probably won't help.

"You are all so beautiful, lovely customers, we have so much in store for you," he says, repositioning the blade. "We would be nothing without you. You make us." More freestyle. "You give us life, meaning."

No one even notices the ridiculousness of his words. In Japan there's no way to over-thank someone.

That, and they couldn't care less what he says, if they hear him at all.

He looks to *outside person* blondie Sakura, but she's still staring at the ground.

How is it that she's not staring at him?

Does she encounter other *outside people* elevator drivers every day?

Where did she get this discontinued perfume?

Getting away from himself.

Jesus.

Coward.

Looking for any reason to abort?

No fucking way.

Calm down.

My will be done as it is in fucking heaven.

See!

"We hope you've found everything you're looking for, every last important thing, and we promise, if you haven't yet, you will. It's coming. We will not let you down."

***Outside person* blondie remains, still staring at the floor.**

Probably doesn't understand a word he's saying.

It's past nine now, dark, the world seemingly lit from within.

He lets her in the main entrance, gladder than ever to see there's no one around. She follows silently behind him up the stairs to the top floor and down the hallway to his door.

"Wow," she says, standing there. "This is some artwork."

He turns, points at a detail in the wall opposite his door. "I particularly like that corn-on-the-cob guy taking a bite out of that smiling dog."

"It's not what you see, but what you don't see," she says, laughing.

He puts the key in the door, pushes it in an inch then turns to her. "It's pretty humble."

"As long as it doesn't smell like single guy."

He pushes in and turns the light on, waiting for her to comment, wondering if he's caught her well enough for her to recognize herself.

She says nothing, just stands staring at the wall. "What the …"

"I know," he says. "Isn't it crazy?"

"You did this?"

"No, no. It was in the room. I've been living with this babe staring at me for two years now—why do you think I was so instantly attracted to you."

She can't stop looking at herself.

"The paintings in the room are far higher quality than the hallways. People would go nuts with all that shit pressing in on them while they slept, nightmares of onions skinned and skinned and skinned alive."

She turns to him now, wide-eyed, lips apart, her eyelashes looking like they're going to puncture the surrounding skin.

"Sunday night, but …" How to explain? She's waiting. "It's nothing personal … Well, it wasn't, it …"

"'s hard to explain?"

He sits on the bed and she remains on her feet, alternating her gaze between him and the wall. "From an early age I was able to draw. I went to an arts high school, won school competitions, *showed promise.* Realism was my thing, but reality was getting harder and harder to look at. I wanted to paint what I thought people need to think about and be aware of, so I started painting from photos on the Web of environments destroyed, animals slaughtered, people … But it drove me mad, painting *ugly.* The last piece I did, a highly detailed landscape of a massive automobile junkyard, these spent broken forms bleeding sadness and better times gone by, cadavers that won't decompose and give you at least *that*, it took so much out of me. So for four years now I've not really painted at all, only abstract, playing with mood, states. I was going to work on myself, turn myself into …"

She shakes her head back and forth, saying nothing. Speechless, he hopes. There's something to her reaction, almost as if—satisfaction? A gamble that paid off?

"The bathroom is where?" she asks.

"Other end of the hall."

She goes and he stares at his wall of her. He sees it is good. Calling it realism would be a stretch in technical terms, graffiti realism, but it's the most recognizable form he's created since the junkyard. And he's definitely caught her, at least as much as was possible without having her in front of him, without knowing her as he knows her now. He got the eyes right, and the hair. It could be no one else.

She returns and gives the wall more of her attention, then takes his hand in hers. She puts a pill there and tells him to swallow it and he does, excitement coursing through him, of setting out on a road trip with no one to notice you've gone and no one expecting you back. Of a blank canvas and a thousand million ideas of how to fill it. Of a beautiful girl in your room giving you drugs.

She turns off the light and then pulls him up off the bed. She puts her arms around him and they stand holding one another. It feels so good. Just so good. Like he lost his flesh long ago and has been walking the world naked and exposed, cold, the wind and dust getting in everywhere, stinging, but now his skin's back on.

And they kiss, deep, and he wants to get right in, all the way in and out of himself. She undoes his belt and he pushes her skirt over the width of her hips and lets it fall to the floor. She takes off her panties and he frees himself of his boxers. She pulls him to the bed and goes down on her back, legs spread. She presses a condom into his hand and he puts it on, then presses into her and moves, and moves, a gathering storm, waves breaking against a rocky shore, building in force and intensity until, with a blinding wallop of lightning and sizzling crack of thunder, it passes, everything back to how it was, but the air still electric, as if the storm was only prelude to a great tempest that could just last forever.

He wonders who he is, such a stranger does he seem to himself. It feels like he's been meditating so deeply for so long that his old self's been left behind on the other side of an unbridgeable distance. He couldn't be happier for it.

She gets up and puts her underwear on silently, then her skirt and bra and t-shirt. She surveys the scene, the painting of herself on the wall, the view out the windows, then turns to the aquarium in the corner. "What's this?"

"My insect collection."

She steps back from it.

"Bit of an inside joke." He gets up and stands by her. "That praying mantis, see there?"

"Gross. Yes."

"Want to know his name?"

"No."

"It's Hitler."

She laughs. "Hitler?"

"And that one, the big horned beetle there?"

"Genghis Khan?"

"May be, but he's Friedman to me."

"Ummm, okay ..."

"Reincarnation. You come back as lower life forms depending on how close you've managed to come to enlightenment in your lifetime. I figure Hitler must have made his way up from slime by now."

"You're serious?"

Now he laughs, "Of *course* not. It's parable, a bible on the bed stand. But rule one of rational thought, you never fucking know. If these fuckers are those fuckers I don't want them getting stepped on and that much closer to human form." She leans slightly forward to look closer at what's in there. "About a week after Cheney dies I'm going down to the nearest sewage culvert to collect me some slime. Just in case. We've all got to do our part."

He returns to his bed. She watches the aquarium a while longer, then turns to him. "That's about the most absurd thing I've ever heard."

"Well, you've got to get out more then."

She laughs again, then puts her hand to her face and massages her temples a moment, then drops her hands and looks at her feet, wiggles her toes, as if checking the firmness of her stance.

He looks out the window, the trees and electric lines there, the fields, the buildings, the unseen people and insects. Feels the drug coming on strong.

"Well, I better get going," she says, her tone suddenly removed and indifferent, someone else standing there.

"What?"

"I'm off to Okinawa tomorrow with my parents for a week."

6th Floor

[on which reason is called into question]

Did she really *have* to come here today? Wearing *this* perfume?

"Mind your step."

… Some're gone.

… She's not.

!

?

Yeah, right.

At the end of the line we're always still waiting for a Dostoyevsky-esque escape.

But not him. The only reprieve is action. He will carry through with this. Without this carry-through there is no him. No him worthy of mention, anyway.

"Welcome, honourable customers."

To deny reality. So bold and impudent. This human brain, so cocksure, so ready to chase after what it wants. A child that just doesn't listen.

Sakura …

"This elevator will quickly take you higher to …"

Why did she do it?

"Doors closing. Next is the lucky seventh floor with many fine …"

Though he knows now, it doesn't make it any easier to take.

Control, honour: perfect. Beautiful.

Correct knowledge, great.

But mistaken understanding! Like everyone.

Sakura!

桜!!!

His escape. His bubble. His gluttony and his blinders.

This *outside person* 桜 is his sign.

This is it.

There is meaning here.

His last trip up.

He still can't believe she left him like that, high on E and lost within himself and wanting nothing more than what she was taking from him. Why would she? Whether there's an archetypical Japanese character or not, this girl is like no one he's ever met. He hasn't been meditating at all, just unable to, his mind won't stop thinking of her. In fact, he's even had to have a few beers each night just to calm his mind enough to get to sleep, like he used to have to.

Fine, full disclosure: He even got some E from Julie and took that a couple days.

Fuller disclosure: He's an idiot if he doesn't just let her go, drift away and disappear from his mind and heart like a smoke ring out a window; she's too dangerous, too disruptive to his training, this training that has saved his life and given him meaning, a sense of honour and integrity. And this with her is demonstrating just how over-confident he'd become, how weak he still is, how many joints in the structure of his mind need reinforcing, bracing, more bolts and rivets and screws and all of them tightened. This has shaken him, loosened them all. Stripped them, even?

So of course he answers her text when at last it comes like the search-and-rescue plane finally dipping its wings to you. He searched every corner of his mind and soul and there was just nothing there to fend her off with. Lost, the words in his head evaporated, logic bent, numbers piling into one another and crushing the operation signs between them. And he felt, somehow, *liberated*, like a mad scientist finally conceding that his math's wrong and finding there's no ill will against him, just an offer of a nice warm padded room where no one will have to worry about anyone hurting anyone else ever again. And he realises this is the closest to a Zen state he's perhaps ever achieved. And maybe the farthest. Paradoxical symmetry. Reason broken down and a new angle of attack on *Mu*.

And now here he is, flagging down a taxi in front of Sekaido after dropping 50,000 yen on paints, brushes, scrapers, and three two-by-four-foot canvases—one for him, and one for her. A cab stops, he throws himself and the stuff into the back seat after the door opens automatically for him and he tells the driver the address. He gives monosyllabic answers to the driver's questions that form an attempt at conversation, and thankfully, like a geisha trained to know what you want, the man gets the point and gives his full attention to the road. At a red light he watches the people pouring across the road in front of them, a river of bubble universes flowing, some attractive, some very attractive. His left arm is draped over the bagged canvas and he caresses it, but his hand is sweaty and the plastic sticks to him.

They start moving again and he wonders why he's bringing this stuff. A resistance to being consumed by her? An attempt to show off, show her he's more than a pretty non-Japanese face? Is it an attempt to share part of himself with her, to reveal? Even fucking more than he has? At least *some* showing this time, instead of so much damn telling.

He pushes it all away and just thinks of her. Cherry blossoms. He imagines painting her body, dragging the tense horsehairs around her hardening nipples, concentric shrinking circles, getting closer and closer. He imagines dragging them along the thin skin of her inner thigh, smoother than the finest drawing paper, edging higher then pulling back, then up and back again, and again, skirting the issue, then pulling a tube of paint out and dripping it all over her, and another, and another, a Pollockesque masterpiece. And then massaging it all out with his hands. And then …

At her house he pays the driver and gets out. He stands there, watching the highly polished car drift down the street leisurely and then turn left and float away without a signal or a wave goodbye. The hazy night sky shows nothing of what's above it; higher order thoughts can't get through as the underbelly of the clouds reflects Shinjuku's *hara*, a glowing warm reflection of its neon and halogen soul.

He looks to her door, closed. She has not come to open it. Is she doing something other than thinking of him? Not watching out the window waiting desperately? Not flinging herself out the door and throwing herself at him, desperate to have their week of not-togetherness over at long last. Maybe there's a note on the door, in the most beguiling and provocative calligraphy ever set down on paper, inspired by the deepest love to have ever grown out of a tangle of neurons, telling him to just come in and come to her room, where he'll find her on her bed, nude and on her back with legs spread, touching herself, summoning moisture from dry surfaces to quench his deepest thirst, like Jesus turning water to wine, with labial cherry blossom petals spread everywhere and catching so gently the light from the universe of flickering flames anchored to candles—as she waits for him to come and make his point.

He approaches the door and it gives away nothing, just a cold shoulder of frosted glass behind metal bars. He presses the doorbell, which does not click satisfyingly like his elevator buttons, just a rubbery hardness that allows itself to be compressed, life poking dead flesh. And there's no sound either, no sign of life anywhere beyond the door. He hears children playing somewhere and a plane soaring by somewhere high overhead.

Three seconds.

Ten.

Twenty.

Press again?

Press again.

Ten more seconds.

Five more.

And then the door pulls in and there she is. She doesn't even say anything. Just smiles and holds the door open, her left breast pressing against her t-shirt. He walks in and puts his bag down. She says hello but doesn't make any sort of move to hug him, and so he's inside but feels outside.

"What have you got there?" she says, a look of knowing unknowing on her face.

"The fundaments of creation." His pretentious words, which came seemingly of their own will, cause him to snicker, but she's not laughing.

"That might work," she says, then comes toward him and takes his hand.

He's never smoked crystal meth before, but he knows the legend of the scabby rotten-toothed grossly-aged wasters who'd fuck-over or flat-out fuck anything for a fix, but God, is Sakura the opposite of that! They *all* use it, and other drugs, now and then for school, to help them study, she says. That you're okay as long as you keep a handle on it. Harmless or not, when you get right down to the hurting edges of things, placed on foil over flame and transformed into a bubbling liquid then vapour that snakes its glorious grey-white way into the glass pipe that seems to both follow and lead it at the same time, it's the siren call made visible. But it's bombastically barbaric to consider it anything other than in her complete control. And if Sakura is good, won't Sakura-plus-drugs equal better?

Yet he knows he's risking undoing the last thousand days of his life, the most meaningful and deliberate fraction of it, the only time he's ever felt properly on the right side of wrong. But has it not been all unravelling lately anyway? Has he not been feeling stuck, trapped between floors? Despairing of ever finding his way out? And tonight, he knows, something has happened, something in the juxtaposition of Sakura with thoughts of art, himself, meaning, love, guilt shame fucking idiocy; he feels like his infinity of choices has suddenly been condensed down, like his house is on fire and he has time to grab only one thing. He takes the pipe from Sakura and breathes in the life she has created for him.

The high gives new meaning to the word, to the world. It isn't marijuana's welter of random ideas and noticings, but crystal clarity of mind and massiveness of motivation. His mind's his own and his thoughts are clear and precise and efficient, sharp and born of intention, a pleasurable and skilful sidestepping of anything not worth the risk of spending one's last moment of life thinking about. He can't believe it—this is, after all, what he's been training his mind so hard to achieve: a prodigious absence of self-doubt, a brick-like confidence.

A sense of no-need-to-question-anything. He feels like a child standing for the first time, a man in a cave who's just realized that till now it's been all shadows. He'll kiss it all, from shoelace to screeching shoeless shrew, if only it presents itself for exaltation. Every single doubt he's ever had about anything ever vanishes and he knows reason is the home that birthed him but he's newborn now, as unable to go back as a bloody crying baby in the doctor's arms. All that idiocy fundamentally supercilious. His focus on his body, health, control, power, self-absorbed and dispassionate. Fuelled only by anger and fear and a shallow third-person version of love that is never honest and true unless it's in first.

So they paint, and it's like he's never painted before. Almost unaware of her and her her-ness, he stares into the is-ness of his canvas, enthralled by the space, the world waiting to be created and stepped into. Details are so sharp, every weave of the canvas holds more possibility than he's ever before noticed, the side of the weave and the over and under and the buried faces, dimensions folded in on themselves. He's tempted to go realistic, but though he's seeing a lot of good, he's not about to turn away from abstract, the style that allows him to create his own beauty and truth in a world grown too ugly to love.

Yet …

In this moment, like God, when he looks upon existence he sees that it's good, so good, which for him is like stepping into a warm shower for the first time and realizing they don't *have* to be cold.

Life is beautiful when it is.

7th Floor

[on which he knows what direction his shoes point]

"Valued customers, you won't even believe the meaning we have waiting for you on the next floor."

God, but was she beguiling!

Inexorably sexy.

"Some wonder how we do it, but we won't give away our secret. We just know you, we know your wants and your desires."

He doesn't know the middle thing about her wants and desires.

"We know them, because we create them."

No sense of disgust at all. Is anyone listening? Doesn't anyone hear him?

***Gaijin* Sakura, his one ally, still staring at the floor.**

"You will all buy, you will all find things that meet a need, you will all spend money on the next wonderful floor. You will be so thankful. It's what we do for you. So thankful."

And after a month of this he's in love with life in a way he's never known. He's arrived in a place he's dreamed of but never imagined. There's an awareness of playing with fire, but he's not thinking about it. Just as he's not thinking about his training either; he's just riding this today and letting tomorrow have its own space, living in and for the moment. Like a good Buddha. A Zen teacher asks his student what direction his sandals are facing in the vestibule; student says he can't remember and teacher says end of lesson, see your sorry ass next week.

As they wind their way out of Mt. Takao station it's obvious that despite it being a weekday it's going to be crowded. They cram into the funicular that takes them up the first half of the mountain and on this glass-clear day the views of the Kanto plain are long and satisfying. They follow the crowds to the trail to the top and soon they're walking single file through the Cedars in a slinky string of nature lovers all perfectly provisioned in high-end hiking bling—backpacks, boots, hats, poles, everything. The measured monotony of the garb matches the replanted forest, which is a garden of soaring trees irregularly patterned but evenly spaced and with very little undergrowth, yet it's oddly beautiful, so tidy and efficient, so considered.

They don't say much to each other on their way up, taciturn as the trees, and at the top they weave through the crowd and find a tight place to sit beside one another, surrounded by others looking south onto the snow-clad-still Mt Fuji—Fuji san, 富士山—rising up out of the swelled plain as if all elevation for miles and miles has been put in one place, all eggs in one basket. He suddenly wants nothing more than to be alone with Sakura and he wonders if they shouldn't have gone to the beach at Enoshima, maybe even Chiba. But the Zen man never regrets a choice he's made, and Will intends to never regret a thing again. And as Sakura hands him his hit of E and he tosses it down his throat, he knows he won't regret this choice either.

"Wow," Sakura says, putting her head on his shoulder.

"Have you ever climbed it?" he asks her.

"No. You?"

"No." It comes as a surprise to him that he hasn't.

They sit a while longer in silence, and then he feels the energy coming, the flow of the high, the warming wave that washes disinterest and boredom into a fifth dimension, and he wonders that there is a single argument against this because he can't think of any, none at all. He looks at Sakura but she's looking down to the restaurant area. A man is leaning over a railing, dropping crumbs or seeds or something to the pigeons below, who fight beak and claw for it.

"Imagine," she says, "living in masses like this, never being able to store food away for later, in a world chock full of worthy competitors." The words sound odd to him; there's an academic remove, an absence of emotion. And the words are the most his that he's ever heard from her.

She says nothing more, so he has a go at sounding like himself. "You start to feel hungry, then you start to bonk, and there's no reserve. Find it before your energy wanes completely, or there's you, completely waned, for good."

"Waned for good, love it," she says, still looking at the birds. "You do have a way with words. *My* words."

He wonders. Japanese. *Nihongo.* 日本語. Japan language. Language, that technology that made and makes humans human. Gives us deep consciousness and ability to connect to others. This *is her* language. 桜の言語. Who is he to be speaking it? Thinking with it? What made him want to learn *this,* to express himself this way? What the hell was wrong with English? Did he think this was a good way to remake himself and his world? He feels a swelling of pride, of love and respect for how amazing we humans and our capabilities are.

The man's out of food and the pigeons disperse and set to scavenging amongst the crowd. A smile comes, a desire to laugh, a sense of rightness, of not-wrongness. Beauty. And subjectivity and a choice. Above-it-all-ness. There but for the grace of God; there but for *my own* grace. These birds are absolutely idiotic, desperate, like robots, none of the art and sensitivity and intelligence that humans have. Step on one and no one will care. Smash it to feathery wet smithereens and it will have no more effect on any emotion or sense than turning out a light or kicking a can down the road.

"So, what now?" she says, turning to him and holding him tight.

"What *not* now!" he says and gets up and pulls her to her feet and takes her head in his hands, her glorious black hair flowing through his fingers, the most complex system in the universe between his palms, the most efficient use of energy, a million zillion calculations a second, this, perhaps the most beautiful iteration of it. He kisses her and then hugs her, staring out at the distance. A scarred wall of stacked storm clouds is folding in on the eastern Pacific and he feels the need to go to it, get off this mountain and go greet the sea. Get away from all these people. "We need some isolation, Sakura. Angry waves and empty beaches."

She offers no argument and three and a half hours later, after stopping in at Ito Yokado to buy some warmer clothes, they're sitting in the sand on the dark windswept beach, gloriously alone but for the careening seagulls, so much more majestic and presentable than the pigeons, and the odd soul wandering past.

A particularly heavy gust of wind shakes them down and Sakura shivers, draws her jacket up tighter to her. She looks off to the horizon, then is forced by the wind to bring her gaze back to the earth at their feet. He looks out at the sky. It's bruised, but blue's still visible in patches over waves standing tall and baring their chests. They watch an old man walk along the edge of the surf, a little Pomeranian pulling dead ahead assiduously on the end of a leash like a kite.

"So, *Will*," she says. "You're named after intent, human capacity to act?"

"Actually, it's a short form. For Willard," he lies, laughing.

"*Weerardu*?" she says.

This makes him laugh all the harder. Thinking of having such an idiotic name, and being in Japan with it where it would be pronounced so incorrectly, an idiotic name further idiotized. "Wow! A rose by any other name indeed!" he says. "What would I make of myself if I were a God damned Weerardu!"

She's not laughing and he wonders if he's insulted her. A sobering stress fracture. "No, it's just Will. My dad said it's so I'll always remember I've got to make it on my own like he did because he's leaving me nothing when he dies. He pretended to be joking, but he wasn't." Ahh, the incredible power of particular drugs, to allow him to speak of his father and still feel good! "And Sakura," he says, "the flower of the samurai! Pretty major symbolism there. Selflessness and bravery, and loyalty first and foremost. Is that why you have the tattoo? Do you ever feel the weight?"

"No weight. Not burdensome weight anyway, the weight you want to be carrying because it means you're substantial."

This feels like the most she's given him of herself. Is she truly just slumming in Westernism? He finds himself straining to reply; he's given so much of himself already, it's almost like he has nothing of substance left to give. "Do you realize, in that way, our names match? We're a perfect couple! Samurais master their will, take complete and total control of it, to complete their humanity."

She gives an absent laugh in response. He watches the waves, but the wind's blowing the sand such that it's all he can do to avoid getting it in his eyes. They toy with the idea of going in the water but decide against it. "Wouldn't want to accidentally kill any fascists who've made their way up to jellyfish," she jokes, and he tells her that's exactly right, glad things have gone back to light.

So they get some somewhat stiff tuna sandwiches and *umeboshii onigiri* from a Lawson's and in the low-lit lobby of the first love hotel they happen upon, they pick the cheapest room from the board. Will slides his credit card under the darkened glass and a moment later receives it back along with a swipe card. This isn't one of the cheesy themed love hotels, like Elvis Lives or Santa's Workshop, so their room isn't too kitsch or creepy or funhouse-jarring, just plasticky-slick swank like a seventies porn shoot. At the foot of the bed is a fifty-two inch LCD and at the head of the bed is a console that reveals itself to control the vibrations of the bed and a flashing light show that, with all the mirrors beside and over the bed, lends the effect of travelling through a wormhole, "or achieving enlightenment," Sakura jokes.

They smoke some *shabu*, they eat their food, and they watch the news, which is focussed mainly on Abenomics and his wanting to re-write the constitution to allow for the creation of a Japanese offensive force. He can't stand to listen, not because it pains him, as he knows it should and is thankful it doesn't, but because he wonders why anyone would choose bad news when a channel away there's good. He ends up in the HD porn channels and stops on one showing two hairy men and a young girl engaged in procreation and he feels himself harden.

"It's so sick," says Sakura, and he finds himself again surprised by her.

"Well, yes, and no," is the only honest answer he has.

"Poor girls, reduced to nothing but moans and holes." She takes the remote and changes channels, settling on a sports station showing the Hiroshima Carp battling the Fukuoka Softbank Hawks.

"You watch sports?" he asks her.

"My dad got me into baseball when I was young. Of course I guess you disapprove."

Again, the sense of daggers thrown, and the sense of imperviousness. "I do?"

She turns to him. "*Professional* sports? With the billions of dollars and all that? All the attention not spent on more important matters?"

"Well, there's some truth there. But I like basketball. And F1."

"Why?"

Why indeed. "At least these are people who are intrinsically without question good at what they do and remunerated in a fashion that doesn't involve theft. You don't want any of it, you don't pay for any of it. It's fair. And it's the best of the best. And as far as TV goes, sports are really the only non-depressing option. At least it's people wearing their hearts on their sleeves and not afraid of a few blood stains. Just a will to act and achieve perfection."

Sometimes he even amazes himself. Especially lately.

They wake, smoke, make love again, shower, and then find themselves in the dry warmth under a clear post-storm sky of crisp one-dimensional blue. The ground is still wet in places and the air has the air of a big job done; obviously a storm let loose while they slept, and yet deep in their love hotel with no windows they never even noticed. On the ride north the nearly empty train's peaceful, the endless city sliding calmly by like random thoughts while the sun's untroubled rays glint off every surface, as though every thing is infused with its own light, a will to burst forth and be. Which makes him think of the inherent truth in everything, is-ness. He looks at Sakura, more is-ness in her than she can contain. He's scared to touch it, so he watches. In his mind he kisses her, he tells her he thinks he might love her, because he loves every fucking thing, and more than that, he wants to see the dynamic grace of a change of expression upon her face. But he doesn't actually have to do anything himself, just watch as the world provides her all the stimulus she needs.

Yet a certain greed demands he take some for himself. "I'm worried you're falling in love with me," he says to her and tries to keep a straight face. The change of her expression is to a look of energetic excitement, a flaring of the soul in her eyes, which truth-be-told is inscrutable, but he reads it as agreement and wants an award for having summoned such a thing into existence. A moment later it's dying, a supernova in an instant. But this look is amazing as well, because no matter what her face is doing and showing, it's a vision. Like the view out the window, the way the light shines, the air on his arms, and on and on. And a part of him that cares for some reason knows the drugs are responsible for these loves squared, but that part of him is not part of *him*, it's someone banging annoyingly on the door. He will not answer.

The outside world is part of him, understanding and empathizing. Simply looking at Sakura's face, the meaning and contentment that it provides, the sense that nothing could be more important, every neuron in on the act, all pulling together to show him that perfection is attainable and doable—he's doing it right here and now! Just keep this up! You can! No other than now, other than this! You're the luckiest motherfucker in the world! But you're deserving, because you paid your dues, you took your chances, you're willing to sacrifice the fucking future for now. You've got the balls and the sense and the courage and intelligence and the wisdom and the universe-endowed talents and qualities and beauty! Yes! And you see the art! The art in everything.

8th Floor

[on which he's hauled up out of the water once more]

"Thank you so much, valued consumers, for gracing my elevator with your presence for these ever-so-brief moments that I'll honestly cherish forever."

Is this not too much? No, because he means it.

But no notice on anyone's face. Is he this invisible?

And *gaijin* 桜 girl, still on, going nowhere and understanding nothing of what he says. A fucking waste. All of it.

Maybe she'd like to …

"Valued customers, you won't even believe the meaning we have waiting for you on the next floor."

Is he ready for this?

Is he?

To embrace his madness and set it on fire?

"We know you, we know your needs."

Everyone's ultimately the same.

At root.

"Because we create them."

Again, no sense of disgust at all.

"Believe me, you will adore the next wonderful floor. You will be so pleased. It's what we do for you."

What the fuck is he on about?

He thinks he might laugh.

He can't believe it.

This might be more meaningful than anything he's got planned.

A warm breeze blows slight from the south under a crushingly blue sky punctuated sporadically by cotton batting clouds. Twenty degrees and no trace of moisture, it's not necessarily the perfect weather for catching fish, but it's the perfect weather for trying. Surreality on the Pacific. Sun above and breezes around and crystal meth within, he's got not complaint nor tangent plane. Which all feels like tremendous success of the spiritual kind, though others on the boat are having more of a practical kind of success—like securing food for themselves and the ones they love, primordial directives, evolutionarily engrained commandments being obeyed by the fit. Yet he knows he's a deeper, more robust and fetching sort of fit.

The only sour note, though in a way it's deliciously so, is that he's noticed that upon removing their fish from the hook Sakura and her brother and his friends are throwing them fully alive into their ice-filled coolers. The poor fish are suffering prolonged and painful deaths as they asphyxiate and freeze. They should be put out of their misery. It's the least we can do, if you ask him. But no one has, and even for himself, the thought is somewhat academic and the ugliness fails to get through to him with any feeling. If anything it only feeds his pleasure, allowing him to feel above these others, to feel that he's more sensitive and would never cause such pain and suffering to a living thing. He's an *artist,* after all. All he feels is happy and content, the sky and the sea and this rented fishing boat that bobs along between them are all in on transmitting some deeper than intellectual message to him that all's well that feels well.

After another hour of tossing the odd response out to Sakura and the others who require interaction to avoid feeling weird about the *outside person* who seems to have no capacity for providing for his family, he's starting to feel the ebb of the high. He's just about to call Sakura to ask for some of the E she brought, when from the depths of the glistening green there is a definite tug on his line and without even thinking about it his body responds by snapping the rod toward the sky, which sets the hook, and he begins to reel it in. They're fishing rather deep and it takes some time and effort before he can finally see the silver flicker of light coming up through the water. It's not big, not big at all. Probably not even really a keeper. Just the weight of the line making it feel big. Reaching over the side he takes hold of the leader and carefully pulls the doomed fish out of the water, wishing it would put up more of a fight, something worthy of Hemingway, if not Melville.

Just about a foot in length and skinnily thick, he lays it on the floor of the boat and holds onto it with a dry rag as he removes the hook. With the fish squirming frantically under his weight he finds himself at a loss for what to do next. He can feel Sakura's eyes on him, watching to see what he'll do. A bit of anxiety now cutting through. Throw it back and suffer castigation from these who seem to consider nothing that might provide an ounce of protein worthy of granting a reprieve. Keep it and chuck it in the cooler and risk hallucinations of tortured fish haunting his every high from now to high water. Or do what his gut tells him is at least a third of the way to right. He knows it's his place in the food chain; killing and eating this fish is completely natural. If he were to inspect its stomach contents he would find the remains of other, "lesser," living creatures, which it had found fit to devour and remove from the land of the living with no regard for how much physical and emotional pain it was causing for individuals and families and communities. And when it comes to this kind of killing of one's own meat, it may seem bloodthirsty and vicious, but at least he's doing the job himself for once instead of just going to a supermarket. Whether it's animal or plant, everything he ingests in order to survive was alive before it was killed by someone other than him. This one he will do the honour of killing himself. And he won't pass the buck to a cruelly cold Coleman Cooler. He will honour his adversary. And they will meet one another in the time beyond and hug and share a drink in the way that only the honourable are capable of doing. In the grand scheme of things, this fish is lucky to have lived a free life up until the moment he died; so many harsher fates await fish and man.

Now he's pretty sure he could never even consider doing this with a land animal like a rabbit or a deer, but fish seems easier somehow, their bodies less expressive, and they're wet anyway—the blood is not such a shock. And fish have a perpetually sad look, as though they're already fully aware of how cruel the world is and expect what's coming and even thank you for proving them right, muscularly opinionated philosophers of the waters that would rather die than be proven wrong. This makes him, momentarily, want to laugh and throw the fish back even more, just to fuck with his mind, but he looks to Sakura, busy casting, the hardness of her jawline, the fucking sexiness of it, and he shakes his head and laughs at his ridiculousness.

The fish wriggles.

He decides to cut its head off. At least it's sure to be quick, and relatively painless.

Putting on his samurai mind—and the airs of one who knows what he's doing—he takes the knife in one hand and presses the fish against the wet floor of the boat, hard. He's barely twisting now and he tells it to be thankful it was caught by such a sensitive guy; this is no walk in the park for either of them. And the ridiculousness of that registers somewhere within, but it's too deep to hurt. He looks and sees Sakura's brother watching him out of the corner of his eye; perhaps his own guilt is serving as explanation as he says not a word.

He takes the razor-sharp, obscenely serrated knife, and places it behind the silvery fish's silently and futilely grasping gill. This is it, do or die; better yet, do or don't die. Silent fucking screams all right. He feels vaguely nauseated, his heart racing and warm drops of sweat trailing down his back. The *shabu* effect is gone like it was never there. Maybe even drugs have their limit; there are things the brain takes seriously and no drug can throw it off the scent of? This thought scares the hell out of him and he worries that he's having an anxiety attack. He launches a series of laughs in an attempt to beat it back, and that seems to help somewhat. As the hot sun beats down on him he's aware of every sound: the other guys chattering, the few seagulls in the air scavenging for sustenance, and the gentle splashing of the waves against the hull. His senses are become hyper-sensitized, like the way they say some people find superhuman strength in life-and-death situations. He's one with this fish at the moment of its death; his heart will stop with its. He's the executioner and the condemned at the same time, like he supposes is always the case.

As though someone else has taken control, he weights the knife and takes a deep breath and as fast as he can he begins to saw through the fish. The rigid condemned tenses under the iron grip of his hand. Tenses, flexes, flexes, but his grip is firm and infallible. He will not screw this up. The knife meets no resistance at first, then the hard density of the spine. Tenses, flexes. Mad panic. He cuts right through it and now the knife is grating away against the floor of the boat. The head is lying inanimate, forever separated from itself and its family and this world. There is more blood than he expected, if he expected anything. Violent. Ugly. Crushing. He feels as though he's just destroyed all that is good in the world and himself. And after a moment of numbness calmness reigns, as if he himself is experiencing the timeless nothingness of death, of no-sense, of not-alive, of not-anything. And it feels good. Like a decision has been made and there's no need to lose sleep over anything. Like what is has finally been proven to be *is*, and let's just grow the fuck up and man up. And then it feels bad. Maybe the violence of his act is the evil? Wouldn't the fish's family be less haunted if their nightmares were simply him freezing to death over ice, versus being massacred and overpowered and belittled and emasculated and deformed and *defeated and insulted and fucking tortured forever*?

He snatches the head and throws it into the ocean. His left hand is still clamped around the rest of the body, which continues to flex as the last instincts of life ebb away. He feels like he's just pulled a gun on an empty closet, on a mirror.

Or maybe the emptiness has pulled the gun on him.

Sakura has disappeared. Maybe gone below to have a drink with someone. Left him alone with his battle. Or was she embarrassed, confused, fucking ashamed. The drug has bled out of him and he's in shark-infested water with his cage broken apart and on its way to the ocean floor. A sharp edge of it cut his side as it slid past and there's blood in the water. He needs Sakura's E. Right now.

Blood on his hands that needs to be washed off.

But Sakura and the E first.

He calls her in a voice that sounds loud enough only for the dead fish, now one with everything, to hear, but she's right beside him. God she's beautiful, and she's smiling.

"You got one," she says and he nods. He sits back on the bench, the sun too hot. She has a beer for him and it's ice cold. He takes a long pull.

"You have quite a way with that knife. Scary." She pinches him, then hands him another pill and they each swallow one down. "Truly a white guy samurai."

Holy fucking beauty of a dig! Or just a joke? Or sincere?

He's as lost as he's ever been for words, for understanding, so he just closes his eyes and lets the largest body on earth comfort him.

As if sensing his anxiety, she sits silently beside him, holding his sticky hand. He opens his eyes and watches her watch the waves. She looks to him again and smiles, then looks back out at the sea. And he understands something but isn't sure what. He digs at it, wonders; when she looks at him, does he see any love there?

Is that it?

He cannot produce love in her?

Blood in the water.

Jesus, hurry the fuck up, E! Emergency here!

He feels bled out and empty. Empty and alone on a boat on an ocean. Cast away?

How?

By who?

Thoughts of his *family*. His *mother*. Guilty, but only by association? A realization that no one has ever looked at him as she did, with that love, like nothing he could do would ever destroy it, he *would* be *understood*, understood better than he understands himself, absolutely unconditional, like every single last little thing he is pleases her in a way no other single last little thing can, like God looking on his creation and seeing it is right. He's never got that from anyone else. Depresses him, family first always, why the wealthy can impoverish so many without caring, and it's ultimately self love. Loving yourself in your progeny. Disgusting! God is this day fucking with him!

But Sakura's holding his sticky hand. She's here with him. And this sea and this boat on it are holding him up, and the sun is warming him, rays travelled in literally the greatest possible hurry just to soothe him. He feels a smile coming to his own face. The drug at last. The anxiety falls away and he feels like he's been pulled up and out of the shark-infested waters and onto a luxury yacht, a pina colada placed in his hands, a beautiful woman in a bikini wields a wand and heals the wound in his side and seems to take away all capacity for pain.

This is the good—all of existence looks at him with love in its eyes. And he will remember this, he will not forget how to do this. And he looks out over the fertile sea and tells himself there's nothing his eyes can see that he won't now be able to see the bright side of.

9th Floor

[on which you're all fucking nuts]

"Welcome valued customers, those who've been with us from the beginning, and those more recently joined. Enclosed in this box you will find yourself privy to many fine perfumes, shampoos, and underarm deodorants."

Is he pushing his luck now? Was that a giggle from one?

Pushing his luck?

Gaijin 桜 still staring at her feet, blond bangs covering everything she's got.

"Shopping. Shopping. Shopping. Gathering berries, aren't you all? Yes, while the men are out hunting, you're gathering, providing ninety percent of the sustenance."

Now, a guy, a foot shorter than him, but looking at him, apparently noticing his snark, if that's even what it is because he's not sure. He's got a beard, so atypical on Japanese men. Maybe that's why. He's a fucking caveman, noticing the dig on the company line. He wants to crack his skull open and feed on his delicious brains.

"Next is floor 10, but if you want some advice, I'd recommend you skip it and go all the way to 16, where you'll be so high above the city, you might see things differently. And who knows what ideas you might come up with."

All individual shoppers in this load. No one talking. All staring blankly ahead. Not a hint of recognition on anyone's faces. So practiced.

Except for *Gaijin* 桜, still completely convinced the floor's got something better to tell her than he does.

And beard boy now stealing glances down the blouse of the 50-odd-year-old beside him. But, to be honest, her breasts are doing an exquisite job of tent-poling her blouse and creating a gap, that nurturing maternal draw.

Mother.

母.

For their two-month anniversary, which she doesn't acknowledge and Will's too embarrassed to mention, on his urging, they head to Kamakura, the world's fourth largest city in the 1200's when it was a rival capital to Kyoto. Though now consumed by the cancer of concrete swelling the Kanto plain, Kamakura's a particularly pretty corner of it and home to many Zen Temples, including one of Japan's most important, Engakuji, whose wood has not rotted, bowed or gone to termites in the seven hundred years it's sat here. Will's been to this temple many times, loving as he does the intent behind its founding, which was to recognize the honourable who'd died in the great Mongol invasion attempt, the honourable from *both* sides. Because as far as Zen and the temple's founder Regent Hojo Tokimune were concerned, affiliation is irrelevant; in battle and love and life in general, as long as your intentions are pure and you act with integrity and honour, you are worthy.

"Those without such traits?" he says to Sakura, "Well, better watch out for reincarnation; it can be a bitch to the self-loving spineless."

But she already knows all this, and tells him so. So they sit in the shade watching the 人々 strolling amongst the pillars that hold aloft the many-layered manta ray roofs of the main gate, and as he tries to think of something she might not know, a mosquito lands on his forearm and he crushes it.

Sakura throws him a smile and an interrogative look and says, "You know who founded this temple, but you don't know the fundamental imperatives of Buddhism?"

"It's my way of helping. I'm willing to sacrifice the quality of my own reincarnation to hurry up their rebirth as humans."

She shakes her head and turns away so he doesn't go on joking about how he's a changed man now, and how he's going to set his prisoners free in his room, set them free to die.

"Reminds me of a play on words one of my old English teachers told," she says.

"Oh?"

She turns back to him. "What's the difference between a mosquito and a fly?"

"Well, there are a few, no?"

"Sure. But the most important one."

"Umm …" He's trying to think of something witty. Any damn thing to prove his worth. But there's nothing.

"A mosquito can fly," she says, "but a fly can't mosquito."

He laughs, but she only forces a smile.

"And then someone in the class made up their own. A Japanese can *rush in*, but a *Russian* can't Japanese."

"Ha. Like …" He tries to think of another, but can't. At least his mind feeds him something: "Well, a Canadian also can't Japanese, but a *Japanese* can't *Canadian* either," he tries.

"I'm glad you get it," she says, then gets up and heads toward the exit. He reminds himself he just has to get used to this side of her.

After slurping down lunch at a calculatedly dilapidated soba house, he's feeling antsy. "Don't you have anything?" he says to her.

She looks at him doubtfully. "I was thinking maybe today we could try to … We've been indulging a little too much. I have to start seriously prepping for school soon, you know."

A feeling of drifting away. He wonders if she's been using it in between their days together like he has. "How about we start that tomorrow?"

The look remains on her face a moment longer, then is replaced by a smile that one could read as condescending, but he doesn't, because he knows how to survive this.

She pulls out a little bag of pills and he's relieved.

"Better to have drugs and not need them than need drugs and not have them?" he tries.

They swallow the E, pay their bill, and then head for the beach, where they add their red square to the patchwork quilt of blankets and towels and sarongs serving as bases for numerous groups of nearly nude nymphs and their affectedly cool courtiers. After sitting some minutes almost laughing at the beauty, Will can sit still no longer. He gets to his feet and walks toward the water's edge, the breeze of the ocean caressing his inside and out. He's never realized how good the air can feel on the back of one's neck. He's never realized how amazing it is the way sand gives way to one's weight but never completely caves under the pressure. And he's never realized his jaw's tendency to clench, as if in training to deal with something monstrously tough.

This night he comes to learn that Sakura, along with the entirety of the Japanese people, is insane. He's seen traces of it, in the not-angry facades of the packed-tight people stuck on a train stopped dead between stations, in the lack of discontent in his students as they described daily lives of leaving "home" at predawn and returning post-sunset, in the lack of space and the maddening scarcity of real darkness or real light.

They've just finished making love and, lying on the futon in the perfectly clean and tidy hotel room, he revels in the gentle scent of the straw-mat flooring and their sex and her perfume. He can hear the wind trying to steal the beauty from the trees, and over that he can hear her calming breath, regular, denying change and glorifying the dream of eternity. She's staring at the ceiling, her legs spread and her pubic bone pressing hard against the inside of his knee, his arm across the softness of her chest. Head supported by the doubled-up pillow, he looks at her perfect profile, her blunt nose asserting nothing, leaving it up to her eyes to do such work, which they do with the prowess of a master, wielding their cutting gaze deft as a samurai. He's been noticing that the lines of her face are becoming ever sharper lately, her breasts lighter, her ribs starker; she's losing weight without trying, as is he. He tells himself they only look better for it.

"Will," she starts, "I'm afraid this is going to have to be it." She says it in English, the first time she's ever used his native tongue with him, so he assumes the words to be of import. Her tone is grave.

"What?" he says, also in English, hoping almost that she's going to say that they, the two of them, together, *together*, have to quit the drugs. Because he knows they do. He's pretty sure she's got a plan. As for him, well, he's not worried, and he's pretty sure that isn't just the drug talking.

She keeps her eyes on the ceiling and continues on in her own tongue. "We both knew from the start that this could only ever be temporary."

"From the start? Temporary?" He says it aloud in English, an attempt to understand, but the words sound as foreign as an alien language of squeaks and gurgles, stabs and slash gashes.

"My parents won't allow it." She's back to her Japanese now, as if having decided the English didn't fit. "*I* won't allow it. You put it perfectly yourself," she says, looking him fearlessly in the eye. "A Canadian can't Japanese." She then looks away and speaks words not her own to the shadowy ceiling high above:

"*We can't share the admiration of the Europeans for their roses, which lack the simplicity of our flower. The thorns hidden beneath the sweetness, the tenacity with which she clings to life, afraid to die, preferring to rot on her stem; her showy colours and heavy odours—the opposite of our flower, which carries no dagger or poison under its beauty, which is ever ready to depart life at the call of nature, whose colours are never gorgeous, and whose light fragrance never palls.*"

Her body, her presence, feels changed beside him, out of reach, like the forever mass of a train the moment its inertia is overcome and it starts to pull away from you; you can chase it down the platform, but you're never getting on it. It isn't sadness he feels, and it isn't hurt, or even pain. It's anger. Only ever anger. Stronger than ever. It has never been love and he's known it, tried to be happy for it, tried his best, he believes, to ensure it, but now that only intensifies his anger. Overwhelming, roiling, bursting. This knowledge that people will always think themselves distinct, always us and all them, unable to get inside one another, an eternal struggle to prove one's self better cooler deeper smarter stronger tastier funnier sexier hipper than the rest, never seeing that the only outcome of such a state of affairs is a tawdry shallow comfort, a lonely desolate life among the dead and the dreary detritus of the battle. Is the human mind, so supposedly "highly" evolved, destined to just get dumber and dumber till it destroys itself?

And the opposite! Living for other fucking people! Obligations to some fucked-up sense of duty and alignment. Why not just live? Why not just strike out for what feels right? If it's not hurting anyone? Why the fucking hell would anyone want someone they love to do anything other than follow their muse?

But more than anything, the anger is directed at himself, for his dereliction of duty, of responsibility. Surrender to the so-licentious siren. The fucking India-ink-haired soil-eyed psychopath who he sees now has been using him from day fucking one. A goddamn boy toy. A goddamn holiday romance. A goddamn wide-eyed *gaijin* grasping for exotic oriental meaning and belonging and culture and hero worship. Some fucking samurai!

Speechless, he slides his sunburnt leg out from between hers, feeling her pubic stubble.

Scratching, if not cutting.

He has to repeat the destination to the cab driver. "それは問題ありません。私はたくさんのお金を持っている。私は約束する大きなヒント." The driver seems satisfied and the meticulously polished car defeats its inertia with gentle grace and finely tuned finesse. His mind, on the other hand, is lashing out madly. He leaves it on its own to do its thing and slinkily separates from it, a child creeping away from his parents fighting again. He stares out the window and watches lights and reflections and shadows and absences fold over and into and out of one another. Existence. Concrete reality. The world of things. Out there. And before long they're exiting the highway and the heights and density of buildings is increasing, growing increasingly unavoidable. He smiles, just to try it on, and it does make him feel better, but his facial muscles grow tired of the puppet regime and easily overthrow it, settling back into lax complacency under the oppressive dictator that reigns by default.

And then another highway, which lifts off the ground and becomes mostly bridge that weaves between the schizophrenic architectural styles of the buildings that make up Tokyo, and as he watches the light and darkness battle one another, with his mood flowing like water to the lowest elevations, he feels like he could kill. And as he thinks of how the masses, rather than fighting for the betterment of mankind, fight for the betterment of only their kind of man, he wants to kill. And as he thinks how he's hardly better if at all than any in those masses, he wants to kill. He wants to, he can taste it, he has the black-hooded head of that fucking rapist torturing child killing ISIS fucker in his left hand and he's in his ear in a universal language telling him he is evil and ugly and an embarrassment to everything that is beautiful in this world and death is not good enough for him but he plunges the knife into his neck anyway because he needs to and he feels the body tense and quiver and tremble and the hardness of bone on his blade and the wetness of blood on his fingers and the delicious transmission from the body saying it's tasted true reality and seen there are no heavenly virgins or even heavens at all and it was all a mistake and good god how I wish I could do it all again *please* but I realize I can't and god how I fucked up so bad and knowing his loved ones are destroyed in the same moment and knowing there is no redemption and there is no solace and there's nothing but this eternal pain and guilt and awareness of ugliness and mistake and shame and guilt and he keeps hacking at the bone and then the head is separate from the body and he wonders if it was all just a dream, if he actually affected anything, if it wasn't all a big mistake, if maybe all he's done is join them. If it's not his own head he's holding in his hands.

Home again. Huffing and feeling fucking better and better. Listening to old Ladytron through his headphones and staring down the Sakura on his damn wall. He can feel the way she can't stand the sight of him and he can't stand it any longer. He pulls out his paints and wants to find a gallon jug of black he might have forgotten about, but all he's got is endless partially-filled 500 ml tubes of his favourite colours. So it's going to have to be a ragtag peasant revolt. And so one tube after another he squishes empty on the wall and brushes out to a thick bloom of colour that hides what's beneath, like abstract bullshit, the only requirement consciousness and crude mechanical movement, and he repeats and repeats with tube after tube until his wall's a blurry field of innominate flowers burying Sakura and her bullshit cherry blossoms and roses and us and them and filial and cultural loyalty and he takes another huff and it's not enough, nothing is enough, and he thinks of going to Shinjuku and finding an after-hours bar and picking up someone sophisticated, someone not ruled by external expectation, a woman that is her own person, not letting her fucking father do her thinking for her and telling her what not to read and stuck in a racist rut worn in over the centuries by bourgeois progenitors. He looks at his bed and considers for a moment how rewarding it would be, truly, to jump from a high place, relieve every muscle, every bone, every cell and every neuron of its fucking dull unrelenting drudgery. Or, just lie on the bed and try to sleep—his mind might get no rest, but his consciousness will. And suicide's probably best done on a foundation less flimsy than a whim. He forces a laugh and lies down and has a go at sleep and finds that, on this night at least, thank every fucking god that anyone's ever killed in the name of, it's something he's capable of.

10th Floor

[on which art is asked to be Art again]

People come and people go and she's still with him!

"Welcome, welcome one and all. So happy to have you on this voyage."

Guardian angel? Spirit guide? Escort. Spy?

"The eleventh floor is next and what we have there you won't believe, though the top floor, I have to say, is where your mind will be blown." He says this in English, the words sounding so odd, so out of place here, like swearing in an elementary school. The people crowding in smile, making who-knows-what of it.

"Yes come on in beautiful people, let us fulfill all your dreams, all it takes is money."

Finally! She lifts her head and looks at him. *She* smiles. No, not smiles, *chuckles*. Shared language! Better than sex! They've pulled one over. Almost makes him wonder. Almost.

"Doors closing, my people. Careful. Careful. Thank you."

But his smile's fake. Part of his uniform. And hers?

When was the last time someone smiled at *him* genuinely?

Has he lost all capacity to even tell?

A mother with her sublimely uber-perfect six-year-old holding onto her hand has joined them. The girl is looking up at her mother and smiling, the mother smiling back, perfect, total sublime perfection. It could be Ayumi. At least it would mean she wasn't permanently scarred and he might be forgiven.

He looks to the mother again.

That is a real smile.

Like that of his own mother, so beautiful herself.

But anchored to his damn dad.

His damn dad.

"Yep, twenty-seven thousand, I think. It's the most they've ever paid for anything," he says to Tom as they stand before the Morrisseau in the hallway. "Makes him look progressively cultured to his friends. Not to mention being a sure holder of value."

"Does he even, like, *know*, or *care* anything about aboriginal, well, anything?"

Will just looks at him.

"Fuck, eh?"

"Irony is a corporate lawyer owning this painting."

"No shit."

"Nothing *but* shit. Boatloads of it."

"... Well, at least your dad's self-made, I guess."

What? Tom's half Metis and this is the last thing he expects from him. "Fuck, that just skews him even further in his magical-thinking."

"Come on," says Tom in his practiced condescending way. "I'm thirsty."

They head up to his room, the whole third floor of this Beaches home, and they share their beer, getting on a buzz and listening to music before deciding whether or not they feel like heading to the Garrison, a forever Queen Street streetcar ride away, all the slow way west, to see some hot local band Tom knows but he doesn't. Tom lights a joint and they share it and before long the conversation falls into the mire that is global politics and power distribution, and Will's buzz is going bad. "Yeah, right now, my parents in fucking Tahiti, *a well-deserved vacation*, another one. Probably being served fine food by some local getting paid shit to grovel and kowtow to the people who stole their land."

"One of those all-you-can-drink-and-eat glutton-fests, I bet."

"No, that's low-brow crassness to my parents. And my dad doesn't drink, so they'd think it's a lousy deal."

Tom reaches over and grabs Will's guitar and starts lightly strumming it.

Will looks to the stack of *Adbusters* magazines and feels the heaviness weighing. "We've got to do something, you know. Some kind of ... I've thought of burning that painting. Setting it free."

Tom stops strumming, looks at him now. "What painting?"

"Society's been steered into a structure with rules that say my family is allowed to own it. How fucking insane! Locking it up in a box to suffocate and die anyway, only our eyes to feed it. Starve it. We should do it, burn it, show everyone how absurd it is that I or anyone should have this power, this stupid *freedom* to commit such a crime without having to worry about being punished! Destroy a piece of pure art, because I can."

"Oh sure, that would prove lots. A fucking white guy burning his Morrisseau. I can see it now."

"We need acts of true art that cut through the haze of entertainment, through to the truth, like frost scraped from a car's window in winter."

"The truth is that the truth belongs to the powerful. Always has and always will, Will."

"That's exactly why those of us on this side of understanding have to start settling for a little less than absolutes before it's all lost. Science only disproves. All us liberal humanists paralysed by the fear of making a mistake. We're training snipers to hit tiny targets while *they're* dropping cluster fucking bombs from the sky that turn fifty-seven families into a stinky pile of smoking dirt and guts and portions of torsos! All while celebrities distract us and spew magical thinking. We don't seem to *care* about anyone but ourselves and our Facebook page anymore. Fucking idiots *still* vote for Republicans and Conservatives. Unbelievable the myopia. The rich better be careful, because when the reality bites and the shit hits the fan, with god truly dead, fake gods will be even more dead."

"Will, my friend. Let's just leave it for now."

"For when? ... For *never*, that's when."

"I just think it's a bit more bloody complicated. And you're so damn high and mighty and *judgemental*."

"Fucking hell, Tom. We're *all* judgemental, and we need to be more so! It doesn't preclude open-mindedness. What are we if we don't pass judgement? Isn't that the definition of 'alive'? To judge and act? Are not the greatest minds those that judge with the keenest intellect and see with the sharpest eye—and *act*?"

Tom makes a dramatic gesture of looking at his watch. "We better get going, man, or there won't be much point going at all."

"You realize that's exactly what I'm *saying?*"

"Come on, ass. Let's get out of here!"

"I'm in no mood for Ossington fucking hipsters, Tom."

"Come on motherfucker, we're going. Just shut up and get up. Just stop thinking about that shit." The set of his brow is conciliatory, understanding, and he's almost convinced. Tom has always been a good friend to him, the brother he never had. "The only way to stay sane is to remember that man is driven insane in today's world, and keep that in perspective. Insane is the new sane."

He likes that. How it explains his madness away in a poetic way. How it removes the burden of guilt. "Well, all I know is I've been sitting around too long. Time for action."

"Well, don't you dare burn that painting. It may need to be freed, but not by being fucking executed."

"Christ."

The idea came to him while looking at the photos of high places on his friend's Tumblr page. Tony is a "Rooftopper," a daredevil photographer who one way or another gets to the top floors of tall buildings and then stands on or hangs off of ledges to take vertigo-inducing photos of sheer drops and precarious places. When Will called him to ask if he knew how to get to the roof of the BMO building, Canada's tallest skyscraper, he'd said, "As if I don't," and then told him the only hard part is getting in the building, then you just get on the right elevator and then up the right flight of stairs. So he fooled his dad—which was easy; so desperate was he for a ray of hope—and got him to let him volunteer as an assistant at his law office on the 65th floor for the summer. On day three he'd scoped out a perfect storage sight and it took just three weeks of one five-litre jug per day in his gym duffel bag to get the half-barrel's worth that would make a decent point and easy math for everybody. The only part of the plan that didn't work was that Tom wanted no part in it. Only looked at him with a look on his face like he was looking at a painting he thought he understood but now realized he didn't. And worse, couldn't be bothered to keep trying. "At least it's not the Morrisseau," Will had tried.

"You're right, it's what Morrisseau would have valued more than art."

"Don't you see *this* is art, Tom? Performance art for a point?"

"Sacrificing yourself to make a point is fine, Will. But don't be like those idiotic suicide bombers who take a bunch of innocent people with them."

"Jesus, Tom, you've always been prone to exaggeration, but when did you get your Ph.D. in it?"

And Will hasn't spoken to him since.

And so, having lugged the sixteen jugs up in two trips, he sits on his birthday alone atop the Bank of Montreal building watching the afternoon sun working in earnest to achieve its goal of plunging the city into darkness, his mind a swirling welter of wild thoughts that he beats madly back. And then finally it's 5:00. Rush hour. Time. He strangles one last second thought, throws if off the edge of his mind, then starts his video camera, holds his birthday cake up to it and takes a bite, and then one by one he pulls the top off each five-litre bottle of 5W20, the least viscous motor oil he could find, which he figured would translate to minimal flow and therefore thickest coverage, literally and metaphorically, and then dumps them over the edge of the building and down onto King Street, throwing each jug over as well when it's empty. When the last jug is done he takes one of his flyers and holds it up to the camera for a few moments:

This is 80 litres of oil. Or, half a barrel.
If you think this is ugly, Deepwater has spilled probably 5 million barrels.
To match that poisoning, I'd have to do this every day for
Twenty seven thousand years.

The world burns 18 times that every day.

Canadian bank profits last year were
20,000,000,000 dollars and no sense.
To spend this much, you'd have to blow a million dollars a ***day.***

For 55 years.

The richest ***person*** in the world is worth 2.5 times ***that.***
The poorest people have $0.

Ignorance, the root and stem of all evil —Plato

Washing one's hands of the conflict between the powerful and the powerless means to side with the powerful, not to be neutral
—Paulo Freire

He then takes the flyer, puts it on top of the stack of a thousand others, each hand-signed the night before by himself, and drops them overboard as well. He watches the stack come apart as it falls, an explosion of papers twisting and scattering and writhing, a mad blossoming of white upon the shadowy now-dirtier street below.

He sits back and feels good. Damn good. A rush like a drug. A siren now … and now another, rising in pitch and volume, climbing the walls, getting closer. He picks up his cake and eats it, waiting for the police to come, wondering how rough they'll be with him. Maybe he'll offer them some cake. He throws the rest of the cake over too.

His dad hadn't hidden his anger, spewing italicized words at him like idiot, embarrassment, childish, disgusting, idiotic, unimaginable, ingrate, entitled, and on and on idiotically; and then hired the best lawyer to defend him. But Will had refused to play along, would accept no deals, and pleaded not guilty in order to ensure a trial, and then subverted the lawyer's strategy so that he would be found guilty and thus given jail time because he was an adult, having done the act on his eighteenth birthday specifically for that reason. The judge said he wouldn't have given him jail time if it weren't for the throwing of the bottles as well, which put lives in danger and indeed did cut open a woman's forehead and let loose a load of blood. So his dad was livid, especially as it all was such a fall from the high he was on thinking that his only child was at last coming around.

And so he sits silently staring at the table while his dad sits silently across from him. This is his first visit, and hopefully the only.

"I still don't know what to say to you," says his dad at last. "I hardly know how to even look at you."

Likewise, but he's not about to let him get off that easily. "I know your job is to get juries to unsee what they've been shown, but your shitty sophistry's never going to work with me. You'll never get me to unknow what I know, to uncare about what I care about."

"You do understand that you've destroyed me politically? Your own father. I'll never get a judicial appointment now, never mind running for office."

"If I've prevented you getting behind a desk with more influence than you already have, then that's success enough right there."

His dad just looks at him and shakes his head. Will has to give respect where it's due and say it's something that he didn't just walk out after that. "You know, dad, there's one thing I'll never forget you telling me, and I wonder if you even remember it."

"Well I certainly don't remember telling you that if society pisses you off go ahead and dump oil on it and get thrown in jail for juvenile lefty politics."

"I was seven or something, I tried to talk to you about poor people, why we didn't share some of our stuff, I mean at least with those bulb-bellied black kids on TV who supposedly could be saved for only pennies a day. Do you remember?"

"Vaguely."

"You spewed the cliché protestant work ethic crap, how people need to work for what they get, *like* a billionaire trader works a billionth as hard as a farmer on a drought-stricken field or an untouchable cleaning toilets or a child in a sweatshop or sex parlour. … And the worst part, you were all fatherly proud, teaching your son that *crisis* builds character, that modern society has become soft and everyone wants a handout, that if you work hard the sky's the goddamn limit. …" He feels his hands start to tremble, his chest get light, his teeth longing to tear something apart.

"You want me to take all that back?"

"And then you gave me a piece of advice to remember. You said, 'Will, you shouldn't feed stray animals, because they'll just go and reproduce'."

His dad leans further back in his chair, doesn't shake his head, looks at the space between them. His bags under his eyes make him look like maybe he's finally started drinking.

Some of the other visitor/inmate pairs talk loudly, others quietly, rustling and shuffling and chair-scraping on the cement floor, the guards watching from corners of eyes.

"Son, I … okay, that may have been a bit harsh, mea culpa. Do we really want to go into this here? My point has only ever been that you can't look out for everyone, life's never been fair. And there has never been more people living in more comfort ever in history—people just need to give up the entitlement mindset—no one is owed anything, you don't see wild animals sitting around waiting for someone to feed them, to build their shelter for them, look after their kids for them."

"Yeah, the noble wild animals your bank and all the companies it funds is killing, bringing on a man-made mass extinction. Yes, I get it dad, every age thinks they're at the scariest point in history, but never has any one man had the power to control and destroy so much, to be anywhere in the world in a matter of hours, to be able to deliver a relentless message and manipulate the minds of so many, to cause so much harm to the planet. Or, conversely, to do so much *good*."

"Would you believe I do believe *I'm* doing good? I *do* care? And I care about you, son. I care, and I don't know where all your hate comes from."

He shakes his head, dismayed once again that understanding between two people can be so incomplete. "I don't fucking *hate*, I *empathize*, and *too* much. How can anyone *separate* themselves from all those babies dying tonight? How can all those rich manipulating thieves care for no one else? I *feel* for all those twelve-year-olds spreading their legs for old fuckers so twisted that only the extreme makes them hard, thinking that each cumshot is as unquestioningly right as the Big Bang, that as long as they blow their load the end justifies the means because they are who they are. I can't empathize with *them*, because I can't even imagine how to get inside such a head." He's suddenly feeling the old claustrophobia again, the sky pressing down on him, the wishing everyone else was somewhere else.

"I know," his dad whispers softly, so not him, as if walking across a bridge of sand that might any moment collapse under his weight. "Maybe we're all suffering from *present*-traumatic stress disorder. You think you have a legitimate reason to hate. But is there ever one? Think about it. All the far right-wingers, the neo-conservatives you hate, the Tea Party types. Why do they hate the immigrants, the lazy, the gays, the whoever they don't understand? Because in the crucial ways it's easier, and it allows the hater to think they're superior. Hate doesn't, *can't* come from love, it comes from ignorance. Sadness, *sadness*, Will, comes from love. And hate's a walk in the park compared to sadness. You just fool yourself."

"Dad … what the hell—"

"We delude ourselves into ignorance, do it all the time. Love, if it's genuine, will never become hate, but we mutate it so we can have the hate rather than the sadness. It's easier to just be angry."

"Ah, nice, Dad. Now *this,* this is my dad talking. The suave orator, the brilliant litigator, the man who can pick holes in any theory, who can put a mask on and pretend to compassion, partnering up with his juries, empathizing with ideals while imploring them to behold the highest of them all, freedom and the danger of convicting unless absolutely sure, like absolute understanding is ever possible, like there is such a thing as a fact."

His father hangs his head, limp, sighs deeply, then comes back to life. "You may be right about something there—it is easier to destroy than create. So I won't bother pointing out any more holes in what you say, your contradictions. I do respect you, son, and I just hope you'll grow out of this—" He stops himself, realizing perhaps he's stepped on a mine. He seems to be deliberating and Will doesn't know whether it's fact or fiction. "You know, son, that flyer of yours, your quotes there, well, I went online and got a couple more for *you.*"

"Here we go."

"*Socialism is a philosophy of failure, the creed of ignorance, and the gospel of envy, its inherent virtue is the equal sharing of misery.*

That's Churchill … but maybe he's not honourable enough for you, not cerebral enough? Well, how about Aristotle, then? He said *The worst form of inequality is to try to make unequal things equal.*"

And with that he gets up and walks away, and Will refuses to give him the dignity of outrage, the victory of having him fucking scream at him and leap for him and smash his face. So he gets up and summons the guard to let him out. And back in his cell he breaks two of his fingers punching the walls.

11th Floor

[on which he huffs and puffs but the bubbles never burst]

She's leaving. She's gone. No fanfare or flick of hair, no sexy backward-walking stare that says I've got something worth ditching your big fancy plans for.

He must remember his past so as not to repeat it. His running from reality.

His humiliation at his own hands.

The obsession, the soft pleasurable option, his laziness and gluttony, his taking his eye off the truth and the wrong and the real love and the duty.

He must not think of her. Or any other her.

Nobody other than himself. That's the way to master one's self.

That was what the Buddha knew. You're allowed to be consumed by yourself as long as once you've figured it out you give it all to others.

Blonde *gaijin outside person* 外人 ESCAPE not-Japanese-speaking 桜 girl. Gone now too.

Maybe *she* had right knowledge *and* right understanding. Is it really so much to ask?

Should he chase after her?

!

Jesus, if anything proves the rightness of this plan, it's this.

He's sitting. Just limp and sitting. Trying to come up with a reason to do something in addition to or other than. Trying to convince himself to stand up, get dressed and go to the bank, withdraw a million yen and let the money tell him what's worth doing. He shifts his eyes from the floor to his desk. Nothing on it seems to matter. Just random ugliness. Like everything. He reaches for his pack of cigarettes, opens it. Nothing in there but the Bic and foil. He turns it over, the lighter sliding into his lap along with a sprinkling of tobacco. He flicks the lighter a few times. Sparks, but no ideas. Just meth. And Sakura and everything she represents and nothing at all he wants to be thinking about. He pulls out the foil. The dry gritty smoothness like fresh cash. He flicks the lighter again, sets the flame to the foil. He watches the paper backing roll away in a wave of red turning to black then chalky grey to reveal the gold beneath. He thinks of the money he's burning through, what other good it could be doing besides keeping his brain in the business of making waves. Waves he's so damn tired of riding. And how many times over the last month he's been tempted to dip into his parents' supply, set himself up in a nice hotel for a while and revel in the meth for however many days it takes, then force himself off the shit, maybe fly to fucking *Tahiti* or some-fantasy-where, get off the shit. But, no matter how many dopamine receptors he blows, no matter how the high blinds him to consequences or how the low turns him into a self-obsessed cadaver, something in him, something in an untouchable dimension, makes the use of his parents' money more distasteful than drinking a bucket of a drunk Republican's puke.

And denying himself that makes it that much easier for him to live with himself for allowing himself this.

This.

He takes the tinfoil bridge and the little Ziploc baggy of crystal from the desk drawer. As he sets to preparations he feels the black ice breaking around him. And he knows his monkey mind is clearly taking control of him. *But all it wants is for you to feel happy, for you to feel good. Is that such a bad thing? Is it not a waste of luck for you to squander your privileged lot by feeling bad all the time for people that simply have worse luck than you? And look at your big fancy interest in Zen, a form of Buddhism, a belief that Karma is the ultimate comptroller of "luck," that you get what you deserve and there's no sense in trying to trick it. And by suffering one's lot nobly, good Karma will accrue and reward will be had. What the fuck are you doing with all this empathy shit? Isn't* that *the weakness that you must defeat? It's a fucking mental illness. You need help, man. Aren't your* parents *right?*

And then, again, the push-back, the *bull-fucking-shit! We might not be prime movers in the physical world, but we* can, *we* must *control our minds, our reactions. Just because this drug's in control of the dopamine system in your brain doesn't mean you have to sell off every square inch of your soul and immolate your morality! And, for the record—get real! You're not thinking of anyone but yourself here, fuckface!*

But, holding the body of the Bic pen between his lips, three weeks Post Sakura, flicking the lighter under the foil bridge and watching the crystals turn to fog which he pulls into himself, he tells himself he has no control, none what-so-fucking-ever. And 60 seconds later he's fine with that. And with the breathless bleakness evicted, he can view the situation from what he feels is a removed perspective, a clinical analysis, the only one that doesn't hurt.

"Valued customers, come in for the twelfth floor and above, where I truly hope you will find what you're looking for."

He's not thinking of her.

He's not.

He's not.

When he'd first started this job he couldn't stop looking at the 人々, but he tired of them all; they all looked the same anyway. Cornflakes. Cheerios.

Not thinking of her.

"Doors closing, take care. You may have visited many stores, many floors, and your legs are tired and your mind is weary, and you can't return home without finding what you're looking for. I hope, so sincerely, that it will be floor twelve that has it for you."

For a while he'd watched the clothes, the men especially, the slight variations in the cut of a suit: length of sleeve, tightness of chest, width of shoulders. So many things to go wrong.

Not thinking of her.

Swimming in or breaking out of a suit. Nothing worse. Better off in a tank top and shorts.

Not thinking of her.

"But if you don't find it there, I plead with you not to despair. For there are more floors above. Thirteen. Fourteen. Fifteen. And sixteen. If you reach the end without finding it, well, maybe it's time to re-examine your needs."

Which was why he'd taken his three ill-fitting elevator-driver uniforms to the tailor and had them properly fitted. A superficial form of control, but every little bit counts.

He's thinking of her.

Thinking of her.

Her.

But as he toes the box tightly into the corner, he tells himself it's only natural. We can't help but think of our loved ones at the end.

He wakes up around 11:00 after three hours' sleep, looks in the mirror, notices how much his skull's showing, takes comfort that his teeth are still white and he's so far maintained the willpower to not scratch himself and so there are no sores—well, none that are visible anyway—and to honour this luck he swears to himself he won't do it this day. He forces himself to eat his cereal, tells himself it's all over and done with and he's going back to the him of four months ago, but within 20 minutes the entire landscape of his thinking has changed. Though he remembers the minutes-ago him, it holds no sway, the depression and the anxiety scares that him away like a front-line deserter you want to shoot 17 times in the back. And he'll smoke just a puff of the drug, then just another, just enough to lift the fog to find a point in getting dressed, getting to the station and onto the train, then driving his elevator or teaching his English classes, then stuffing himself onto the train home. Then, the home-after-work him blows the fog away with a few giant huffs of the cool electric smoke and he paints all night and does not think about gluttony and culpability and need.

And Sakura.

Well, he always thinks about Sakura, but when high he can take the high road and just be thankful to have been with her at all. When low, though, he craves her like the drug, as though she and the drug are one, life worthless without her. He tries to steer his mind away from thoughts of her by going back to his old stomping ground of the world and all its fucked-up workings, but that makes him even more depressed. When low he can as much see the positive side of things as he can see the other side of the moon, for the drug pulls down the walls of his mind, all his ideals and his philosophies framed and hung upon them. Even his vow to never paint realistically again has become so much paper backing turned to wisps of ash too weightless for gravity to even bother with.

In fact he's building up quite a collection of in-absentia portraits of her. He looks into the eyes he's made and fills in the rest of her face around them. At least he has this. Perhaps this can do. Why does he need her now? He has her, the *her* he wanted. He can remember every view, every angle, from looking down on her from above to peering out over the hill of her shaved pubic mound as he held her between his lips while he looked down the plain of her belly to the shifting promontories of her ribs to the swaying oceans of her breasts and the nipples bobbing there like buoys in a storm, her chin thrust up between the swells like Mt. Fuji and erupting with calls of pleasure. He can hold her forever in his mind's eye, forever as she was when they were. In his stoned dopamine-bathed memory it has a delicious immortality, as does he himself. Which is a fuck of a lot better than living in reality and worrying about things outside his skin.

So he takes another hit and paints her lips on. He kisses them while they're wet. Something's missing. He takes the bottle from the top of the fridge, pulls the cap off and flicks a splash of ESCAPE onto her, a priest with holy water. He kisses the lips again, with his tongue, tastes the oil, pretends it's her lipstick. He takes his clothes off and lies on his back, kisses the painting and slowly drags it across his chest, feeling the wet paint catching on his chest hair, yet more of her rubbing off on him.

And he wakes up a hundred times and every time he struggles to the shores of wakefulness, dripping with the wetness of dreams, he can't believe the way his skin's so convinced. While asleep he's laid flat against the oneness of every moment. He's with Wendy, his girlfriend in grade 8 he hasn't thought about in years, but now alive and of his and of this and wearing a sexy dress that accentuates her hisness and her budding breasts and everything about her as he remembers and loves them and then he wakes up. And then he sleeps again and it's more of the same over and over, Sakura, Wendy, Sakura, Sakura, Heidi, Sakura, Wendy, Sakura, Sakura, Sakura, Sakura. ... How many times can one wake in this state? Isn't there a god that watches over things and says that while a knife jabbed through the neck is harsh, repeated awakenings from the heights of deluded beauty to real ugliness is a fate worse than death. And that makes him laugh. What a joke. Why does he fight it? Why, why does he bother prolonging things? What an idiot he is! Build another mountain and light it on fire! Simple as that! No longer a slave, no longer at the mercy of natural states, no longer slapped in the face by this prime mover argument! You! You are it! Feel tired? Wake up feeling shitty? Sad depressed anxious nervous worried deflated, fuck that! You've got it right there in hand! Light it up and take control! If you were a creator, what kind of people would you want to have created??

Exactly!

But wait!

Is this real life?

No. Duh.

No? *Duh?* You fucking look it up and tell me, what is real life??

Yeah, like I said. Look it up and get back to me. But don't fuck me around. I want some serious thought put into this! Because I've put in my hours digging.

He takes the pipe and the lighter and takes a big huff, sees the light coming in the window, lighting up the new school Monet mural he's plastered over Sakura. And there's regret growing. The meth gets his head in order and it helps generally, but not always specifically. He still feels her there behind it all. And he's happy, but also cockily livid. He thinks of calling her. A thought he has who knows how many times a day, a thought he's resisted to date and will hate himself if he gives into. But this time the urge is strong, he can barely control himself. He reaches for the phone and has it in hand, taps to the phone keypad. He removed her contact weeks ago (and all the photos of her) but he remembers her number like the alphabet. And then he throws the phone to the ground and smashes it with his Bose mini speaker.

Then he takes another huff. And then he pulls out the giant tub of white acrylic he bought two days ago and in mad excitement he twists the lid off and throws it at the wall like a bucket of water on a fire, then again and again, then admires the pattern of perfectly snow-like white splatters now giving in to gravity, and he picks up the four-inch brush he bought and he sets to laying it on thick, and before long there's a white wall, nothing to be seen through it, but he knows what's behind it. Still so beautiful, still so Sakura, still calling to him. He thinks of going and getting turpentine and washing her off his walls for good.

Turpentine?

Is that a message?

Like, he's not going to be able to wash his mind clear of her without strong chemicals?

Whatever!

He takes his hair dryer and plugs it in and dries the entire wall.

Then, in thick black, he paints: ESCAPE!!!

12th Floor

[on which Art's hard]

"Floor twelve my valued customers, please alight here for wonderful kitchen wares, bathroom—"

No her.

No anyone.

"Please, valued customers, come in for floors thirteen through sixteen, many more wonderful items."

For the best.

"Door closing now, be careful please—"

How he remembers her in this elevator, pressing stop. Amazing.

He thinks of his weakness. He's well beyond that now.

Stronger.

With a plan.

A fucking plan that means something.

"This victory lap. We hope your needs will be fulfilled. We aim to please, to leave you wanting for nothing. Always. We will not let you down. It is our duty. It is our honour."

And still this pull.

He's not thinking of her.

He takes one more huff and heads out for some ramen, pipe in pocket. Vegetable ramen. A day's salt in a sitting. He sips sparingly of the soup. Though it's rude, he blows on it to cool it down.

A cat's tongue, as the Japanese would say. 日本人. *Them.*

Not him. 外人. *Outside person.*

He stirs the noodles and they form spools around the chopsticks. The radish and leek twist around in the currents. He thinks of Sakura's hair, how individual strands in the bottom of the shower could look so messy, the random scribblings of a toddler with a pen. But the *group*, flowing in elegant unison from her head!

He can't help it.

He can, he just chooses not to.

That's what he tells himself.

He tells himself he wants to think of her. And so he should.

No. It's nothing to do with want. It's need. He only does what he needs to do. He's in control. Not his mind.

He leaves the restaurant, swipes into the station and climbs the stairs to the platform and gets on the train that's right there waiting for him. A long ride ahead of him, all the way out to Chiba. To Chiba for Ted's fiancé Mia's birthday party at her family's home, right on the Pacific's edge. A meditative hour forty-five later, he arrives at Hyuga and in the station lobby locates a payphone, calls Ted, and his already-drunk friend tells him a driver will be there in 10 minutes.

Ted, already the most steadfastly happy person Will's ever met, has become all the more content with the world and its workings since meeting Mia in the book-signing line at a David Icke convention. Mia is a woman whom no one would accuse of relying on her beauty to get through life; it's her wealthy family, more specifically her father, director of marketing for Hitachi, that soothes her passage. Ted had met this pudgy shrill-voiced little shiver of flesh, fat, bone and confused sense of entitlement, and somehow fallen in love and got engaged—dropping the at least reasonably attractive and sexy Hitomi in a move that left Will and everyone else first befuddled, then in happy awe with renewed faith in intangibles and hopeful for things that are supposed to be but rarely are.

Their romance was not without its challenges, though, for Mia's father had intervened, demanding she leave Ted; when she refused, he'd managed to get her to at least put the wedding off for three months (which gave him sufficient time to look into Ted's slightly better than mediocre family background (his father was a doctor at least (psychiatrist, but a doctor none the less (and his brother had tried to kill himself (it was over a failed love, but the story was that it was due to his shame over the failure of his start-up (which was acceptable enough to Mia's very traditionally Japanese father)))))). Will can't stand Mia, but when he thinks of this defiance of Japanese culture, particularly in contrast to Sakura, it's like a Zen *koan* forcing him to accept the limits of the intellect and logic. And he's left fearful for things that are supposed not to be but often are.

But who is he to be even thinking he knows the first damn thing about Zen? Or Japan, or any damn-where-else? Or Canada? Will of no will, of no control, of an addiction to drugs and lofty ideals, but no action. Action, the very root of Zen, the opposite of his life.

A black-suited man approaches him and asks if he is *Weeru san*. Will replies in the affirmative and the man tells him his name is Fujita, he's the driver, and he should please follow him. So Will trails the trim man out into the night and slips into the rear of a Lexus so polished that it's almost impossible to tell what colour it is for all the light it's refusing to accept. Mr. Fujita closes the door, sealing him into the cow's-skin cocoon, then opens the front door and gets in himself. A moment later the smell of leather is outmuscled by the musky scent of the man's aftershave, as if he'd been at the tail end of a two-day bender when called up for this gig and had no time but to shave and spray.

Will lowers his window and revels in the in-whipping air sucking out the cloying chemicals and replacing them with the beautifully pure scent of soil and plant life and ocean. He focuses on this for the few minutes it takes the car to leave the tiny station and come to a stop at the rear of a three-story house whose windows glow with the cold blue-white of halogen light. Mr. Fujita opens the door and tells him he'll be honoured to guide him into the house and present him to the host, but Will explains that he'd prefer to make his own way in. Shifting his weight foot to foot and looking up then down, it's obvious the man's distraught by the dissonance between his instructions and Will's desire, but he quickly composes himself, tells Will that will be fine, and then heads off alone into the rear of house, relying on the philosophy of the customer's always right. Another car, a Mercedes, pulls up, and discharges three Japanese twenty-somethings all dressed up in sharp-pointed shoes, slim-fitting dress pants and wildly patterned collar shirts, bellowing and hooting and hollering as if making sure everyone knows there's no worry of them taking more from the party than they're bringing.

He turns from them and in the weighty throb of the thrust-and-sway-by-numbers dance music pulsing from the house, walks the length of the driveway and through the elaborately-embellished-with-wrought-iron-and-winged-alabaster garden and over the grassy bluffs toward the ocean, well out of sight of the few people outside. On the beach in front of the house a cadre of carefully-dressed people are sitting around a bonfire and a couple of girls in calculatedly short shorts and precisely-tight t-shirts are thrusting and swaying to the muffled beat. The Pacific is lapping shore about a hundred yards out and a two-thirds-full moon is high in the empty sky, looking bored and lonely.

He walks till he's sure he can't be seen, then sits cross-legged in the cold sand and makes his back erect, then pulls out his pipe and takes a few huffs, then puts his cupped hands in his lap, stares at the light 20 yards out into the water, and concentrates on the feel of his skin on the air, of sitting on top of the world on ground that will be under water in a few hours as the water blindly obeys the moon's command. His surroundings fade into the blackness that isn't the light, his nose is becalmed by the perfectly benign scent of salt water and damp sand, and his ears take in the bass and the gentle lapping of the waves that's all the world's greatest ocean can summon to throw at the obstinate land. But his brain won't let go of Sakura, the pea if not the bed of nails his entire existence now rests upon.

Then he senses someone beside him. A girl. *Gaijin*. An *outside person* from out of nowhere. She's wearing tight dark jeans and pink Converse, a plain black hoodie covering the rest of her, long straight brown hair hanging off her head. She doesn't look at him or even face him, just assumes his exact posture and stares out at the water. She's silent, seemingly intent on waiting for him to make the first conscious connection. Within 30 seconds her back rounds and she turns to face him, smiling ironically, and he sees it's Sue.

She really is beautiful. The whites of her eyes are cooked egg, not a crack in them, almost tiring to look at. In the centre of that white are rings of the lightest blue surrounding big black pupils; these blue rings look troubled, as if still not convinced that one day the darkness inside them won't overwhelm them completely. Her face is blemish free, as if never used, never even introduced. Two-dimensional; if he were to paint this face no one would believe he hadn't embellished.

"You a bloody Buddha yet?" she says, punching him lightly in the arm. "Even Buddhas can take a break to have some fun now and then, no?" Her accent is pure American Midwest, Minnesota maybe.

"Quite a moonrise," is all he can think to say.

"Probably enjoys rising above such fine music."

"Not hard to make passable electronica."

The sentence sounds castrating even to him and her face expresses her disgust. "This is *Burial.* He's fucking incredible. And it's hardly *electronica.*"

"I just mean …"

She takes out a joint and lights it, takes a couple quick short drags, then one deep one, then passes the joint to him. He takes a long puff because why the hell not and he's not about to take out his fucking crack pipe in front of her.

Knowing she's deeply into music and deciding on fun, he says, "Yes, there are geniuses, but as long as you can halfway play an instrument and you have good music sense and good technology, you can make good music these days. Of course it's easy to ruin it in production."

"True," she says, disappointingly. "There's alright, then there's perfection. You hone your skill, master it, until there's no longer anything lost in the translation, and there you have it."

He's amazed to find himself, somehow, in the enemy trenches lobbing grenades; but they're already on their way, so, "No such thing as perfection, and it's all in the beholder anyway. Skill's a facilitator, that's it. Art lies in the meaning, and meaning is never constant, it exists in context, and context is ephemeral." He's actually impressed with that translation of his thought, though he's not sure it's his thought at all. Fucking marijuana.

Silence follows his words and he assumes that she's having as much trouble processing them as he is. Then she kicks her legs straight out in front of her, aggressive, like drawing twin barrels. She exhales, deflated like a balloon stuck through but not popped. Then she straightens her spine and the words seem to be formed on the intake, "You're not one of those 'Found Art' types are you?"

There's actual anger in her voice and he feels excitement rising. Is this not to be just another conversation? "You mean like Duchamp? Like the Mutt urinal?"

"Do you *know* art?" she asks, in a tone that implies she feels few people actually do.

Does she? "Somewhat."

"Then, yes, him and all the other abstractivists. How is that art? That's just colours. Art's hard. ... Are you an artist? I had no idea."

"I like to think," he says, excited now, "that everyone is, in their own way. Some deeper than others of course."

She turns to him, whites of her eyes glowing in the moonlight, like moons themselves. "That's crap," she says, as if he's just accused her mother of doing little more than what billions of other women have also done in producing her. "I *hate* that."

"Hate what?"

She brings her legs back into her; readying for another kick? She turns full on him now, thick lips dilated, eyes wide, silky hair going straight south. "Like art grows on trees. Like the label makes it. Rothko with his foggy rectangles, and Mondrian, though at least he had some bloody precision, and, oh God, *Pollock.* Just bloody splattered paint all over the place and he's a legend? Or fucking Richter now?"

He takes another long huff from her joint.

He doesn't know how to say what he wants to say, and she looks like she wants to slap him. He vaguely remembers her telling him she was a painter before, but he'd most likely avoided the topic. He smoothes out his voice before speaking, like ironing a combat uniform. He knows nothing really of who she is. He's never *really* spoken to her. "So the quality of art is directly proportional to the technical skill of its creator?"

"Picasso could draw a line like no other."

Frustration courses through him like waves of nails. He's surprised, but not by the anger that's rising in him. He tries to calm down, knowing it's the fucking marijuana, and that the anger and aggression are his perennial weakness surfacing. "*Love the art in yourself, not yourself in the art.*"

She looks out at the glowing water. Her body loosens, strings untie, an anchor that's slipped. But an edge catches again and she turns to him. "I just ..." Her lines go slack again as she falls silent.

"Why do you do it?"

"Paint?"

"Just art."

She looks confused. "I do it because I love it."

"Like how? Like it's *fun*, to do?"

"Like I'm good at it, and I like it. It's ... meaningful."

"What's the meaning for you?"

She scrunches up her face and purses her lips. "I feel like I'm on fucking Oprah or something."

"You might be someday." There. Hopefully that will earn him forgiveness.

"Well, I don't know. I love doing it. Like someone who loves dancing just does it. Isn't that enough?"

"But why not that and more?"

"Like what?"

"Like ..." Should he say it? Why not! "Like saving the world."

She laughs. Progress, he supposes. "I don't know about *saving* the world, but my work makes it more beautiful."

He inhales deeply of the salty air, then wrestles it into words that sting him. "What about the suffering in the world? Don't you think we have a duty to help in some way?"

"Frankly, no. We all have to follow our hearts while the following is good. You know?" There's an easiness to her voice now. "There's pain in life, accept it, enjoy what you can while you can. Life ain't fair and it ain't never gonna be."

Holy fucking channelling his father or what!

Fuck, he hates marijuana.

He looks up, the moon continuing up and up, brightening but losing contrast, distancing itself, blowing away in the wind that's picking up. He wonders what his face looks like right now. He imagines it would make a good painting. Hers, alive with some weird mordant excitement, would as well.

"It's like people who say they love fucking God. How? You don't *know* him! You only know yourself! So look out for number one. Other than number one, there are only imaginary numbers." Her cocksure expression makes it clear she thinks she has him on at least this point.

She's watching him, waiting, her eyes in shadow under her sharp brow ridge. And he wants to laugh, but he can't.

Slap her!
Punch her!
Self-important-shallow-farthest-from-an-artist-wanna-be-artist! God damn fucking giving-everything-yet-nothing-in-life waster!
Ultraviolence allowed! Warranted!
The sailor who never had any grace to fall from.

Rest now, weary head, you will get well soon.

A silent age passes. "How's Greg?" he says.

"We broke up two months ago. You don't talk to him?"

"I guess I don't."

Then he finds his arm reaching for her, seemingly of its own free will, and he worries about its intentions. He watches as his hand takes her hair in his fingers, feeling the cold smoothness, the floorboards of an ancient temple. He leans toward her. "I do want to," he says, not knowing. He reaches to her with his other hand, puts his palm upon her narrow shoulder and starts feeling her out. It's an awkward arrangement of limbs but she does not resist, so he leans into her and kisses her, smelling the sickly thick scent of marijuana on her breath. He presses his tongue into her, and she meets him. He pushes her onto her back and she does not resist. He undoes the button of her jeans and wrenches them down to her ankles, her underwear with them; they're pink, as if she'd planned on having them around her ankles and wanted them to match her shoes. He wants nothing more than to hurt her, to press into her and remind her she's alive and of a family and to be properly alive and human means to be concerned about more than just one's self, but again he tells himself that that's *his* weakness, that it's for him to find a way to help people without hurting them. Help himself. So he massages her soft flesh, takes pleasure in the sensation of touch and response as the wetness comes, then he presses into her, amazed, as he hasn't had an erection in two weeks at least; perhaps his body has come alive just to spite Sakura.

13th Floor

[on which he has his cake]

"And now, dear customers, please mind the doors as we arrive at the thirteenth floor. Please don't worry about bad luck. No harm shall ever come to you."

He watches those that leave, waddling, strutting, simply walking.

And his mind, the trickster, so creative, proposes a scenario: If *gaijin* blondie 桜 were to step in, having raced up the escalators to meet you here to blow you away, having fallen in love with you at first sight and sound, asking you to meet her at Dutour at the end of your shift, would you do it?

"Yes, please, step to the back please. So many customers knowing good value and quality merchandise when they see it. We will please you all, but please, step back."

No.

No!

No!

Samurai mind.

Never look back.

But what about taking in new information?

"Doors closing. So many incredible and exciting things to be found above. Don't despair. So many options still. We are so happy you are here with us. We are so happy to share with you. God, we love you. We love how you, how you wear such expensive underwear, the silkiness on your softest flesh comforting where you need it most ..."

Come on. Keep it together.

Just three more floors.

It's the third day into his attempt to wean himself off the shit and he'd awoken feeling nauseated, but he refused to allow himself to skip work, as he's called in sick once already from the elevator and twice from this part-time teaching job and he can't risk losing it and being forced to rely on his parents' money and then probably never getting off the shit: a rich white boy junky who hates the way the world works—that sickeningly putrid irony. He'll skin himself alive and bleed to death in a lemon juice shower before he'll settle into such a position. On the train he'd actually laughed, *laughed*, thinking how he could start a magazine, *Hypocrite Monthly* maybe, his smug mug on every month's cover just like Oprah. He thought about how he could include articles by the trendiest psychologists about how to come to love one's hypocrisy, and he could rent scientists for articles on how hypocrisy's evolutionarily beneficial, and he could do exposés on the biggest hypocrites of our times and how they're all famous and wealthy and adored and thus the proof's in the pudding, that COME ON! Hypocrisy's the new integrity! And he could have a monthly feature lauding the most hypocritical politician of the month and why you should vote for him, and sell ad space to pharmaceutical concerns concerned about ensuring that hypocrisy-challenged individuals will know what pills to make sure their doctors make sure their medical insurance covers to solve their problem, and flashy bios on the most hypocritical musicians, and actors, and religious figures. And then sister magazines like *In the Interest of Self*, or *For the Love of Gluttony*, or *Excellence in Exploitation* and and and!

But now, trying his best to focus on five-year-old Ayumi's words, he isn't laughing. What he's doing is trying to hide the quiver in his voice, to settle the twitching of his fingers, to squeeze off the painful cramps that seize his chest, to keep at bay the inevitable doom that presses in on him from all directions. And he wants to kill himself for coming in today, placing this him in the presence of these three perfect and beautifully beatific children. Is this how frivolous the concepts of honour and integrity have become to him? With that thought his mouth starts to water as though the air itself is changing state and his gut's churning, a towel twisting and readying to flick him one monster stinging snap.

And then there it is, all over the table, one massive heave, everywhere, on the kids, who are all too shocked to say anything. And then Ayumi's crying. He looks at her, sees the wet fear in her eyes, the contorted face, green specked by his guts, perfection soiled and defiled, and he wants to fall crying at her feet begging for forgiveness but he can't say anything because he has to fly out of his chair and run to the toilet where he flips up the seat and flings himself at it. Every muscle tenses, like a baker's icing bag about to spell trouble, and he squeezes his guts out of his mouth and it's all he can do to keep his anus clenched to prevent the disgusting sick from coming out that end as well. After a forever of this he pulls down his pants and sits down on the toilet and finally empties out completely. It comes out in one large burst, one massive smack upon the fetid surface of the water in the bowl that splashes up and covers his buttocks in warm chunky wet.

He has to get home, get horizontal, get unconscious. A taxi will kill him for money so he stumbles to the train station, and when the rush-hour crowded-as-hell train comes three hour-like minutes later he presses onto it. He should be able to count on his *gaijin*-ness and the lingering stink of sick to keep people at bay, but when it's rush-hour rammed you have no choice but to face whatever you're up against. Two stops later at Shinagawa he makes it to the washroom, but at Meguro he only makes it as far as the backside of a platform bench, where he wretches and watches the shoes shuffling past, just inches away, knowing the eyes above are all looking down on him, wretched pitiful thing. At Shinjuku, in the toilet of the busiest train station in the world, he again unloads from both ends, then forces himself back up to the platform and onto the final train home, on which, between stations, he begins to convulse in a series of not-quite-dry heaves. He manages to catch the yellow bile in his hands and the front of his shirt, but his body contortions in such cramped quarters result in his having to press against the barely pliant bodies around him, leading to a series of groans and deep breaths; it's as if the entire car full of people are throwing up as one through his mouth. A middle-aged lady with brown lipstick and the silky hair of a 16-year-old asks him if he's okay and he nods and blames bad sushi.

The train finally lurches to a stop at his station and he

presses out the open doors, faint and dizzy, willing himself out the station and down the shopping street, sweating like it's all he has in him. He makes it up to his room on the third floor of the *gaijin* house without running into anyone, though he knows Rick's in by the melancholic music pressing out through the walls in search of company, desperate to escape its own lonely mood. He falls onto his bed and never in his life has he been happier to fall from his feet. Never once. It's the relief of Jesus finally reaching Calvary, able to let the cross fall to the dust at last. As he lies there he's comforted, knowing now that death, in meaning not only the end of pleasure but also the end of shit like this, is nothing to be afraid of. Although he's no Jesus, and his cross is of his own making. And he knows what this is all about: this is honesty, the new hypocrisy, forced upon him by his very own body. He's reminded of his duty, of everyone's. He knows that even a bus driver has a duty, the urinal cleaner and the girl who works at Wal-Mart. In the weakest part of him all he wants to be responsible for is pleasing himself, but he knows few have such a pleasure, only the luckiest and most ignorant of the lucky ignorant.

He's not thinking of her.

Or *it*.

He's not.

He's not looking at the people. Doesn't trust himself.

Too fragile.

This load is talkative.

This one, tired from overuse. Barking orders.

This one, abused. By her husband? Father? Boss? The world itself. Herself.

This one, silent. Talking to herself.

He's thinking of her.

He's thinking of the Morrisseau.

The knife.

The show.

The courage to be summoned.

The beginning and the end.

He used to always listen to the voices, but eventually, like the teeth in a zipper meeting to form a flat line, they'd simply

cancelled one another out, closed lips sealing out insight.

Her.

He thinks of how the one thing he's never been able to shut out, after all this, is the smell. He thinks of how scent carries a world along with it, weightless in the wind.

He's thinking of her.

The gluttonous sink and fester and stink, the honourable rise and refresh and becalm.

Cherry blossoms and roses.

ESCAPE!!!

Her?

For a day and a half it feels like no sooner has he beaten insanity by finding sleep than he is awake again, choking on the smell of the plastic floor and the paint and existence itself, self-induced hell brought on by self-absorbed mental and emotional gluttony. Soul poisoning. Lying in bed knowing now what it feels like to want to die and wondering if it can get any worse, and being pretty sure that it can and thus will, staggering to the shared washroom at the end of the hall to puke and shit (pretending not to be there when on the other side of the flimsy partition a female floor-mate empties her bladder or releases her anus with a swish and plop and the saddest stench), filling his water bottle at the paint-stained sink, falling back into bed and knowing this is restitution.

And then, as the flu or withdrawal or whatever the fuck hell it is lifts, empty hopelessness flows into the space it left behind, and seven out of every eight thoughts are whether or not he should just head down to Julie's and buy some shit off her. No! *NO*—the word itself, the sound and the everything about it, is feeling exponentially more absurd each time he says it. The question itself is becoming no longer one of quality of life, but rather quality of death, and principles are a hard thing to understand in such circumstances, if one actually even ever had them.

Down to Julie's.
Down to Julie's and buy some.
Smoke and be alive and be out of pain and just fuck it all and who cares even just kill yourself by swimming out into the ocean until you can't lift your arms out of the water.
The only way to beat this suffering.
Die high!
No!

And then the intense hunger starts, as if his body has just remembered that it needs fuel to keep the fire burning or else it must burn itself, and then the hunger is unbearable, and in typical body obstinacy, anything-to-win-ness, it reminds him of what death really involves. So he sits up and has some cereal, his head so light it's proof his thoughts are something out of nothing. With the hunger somewhat sated, he comes to accept the possibility that he might *not* die, but that makes him feel no better and he's desperate for anything that might remind his mind that pleasure is something it's capable of.

This craving for the smoke, nothing less than an obsession. It isn't a need, it's a want, and that's worse—for to give in to a need is animal, but to give in to a want is beautifully human, thus to deny the want is to deny one's humanity. He knows this is deluded thinking—he knows that's the problem with the whole stinking human world, the giving in to want. But he *wants* to feel human again, he *wants* to smoke, he *has* to feel something not-completely-and-endlessly-depressing just for just a fucking second, he wants it more than he's wanted anything ever in his life, and the arguments against it are sheer senseless ludicrous idiocy. The world is shit and the word is fuck and people are shit-fucked anyway; to feel non-drug-induced pleasure in such a world is a grotesque madness anyway!

And why, really *why*, why not do it again?
You don't have to be a junkie, just one more god damned time.
Maybe two.

Life is long, the moment is all that matters.
Get you over this hump
And fuck it all anyway!

He goes straight to Julie's door on the first floor.

"Fuckin' 'ell, mate," she exclaims. She's English—very English. Straightened dyed hair, low cut top and everything. But she sounds nothing like the queen. "You ol rite?"

"Yes, I—"

"You look like bleedin' shite. You just crawl out' the ground o wot? I though' they bleedin' cremei'ed the dead ovu''eeya?"

"They don't want to foul the air with *gaijin* ashes so they fly them home. I escaped the cargo hold."

She smiles at his effort, unconvinced. "Really, though, dahlin'. You're a gogeous dead ringuh fo' shite."

It's pretty bad when your meth dealer's surprised at how bad you look. "Just been sick."

"Yeh?"

"I need some."

"Usual?"

"Yep." He hands her the crisp bills.

She turns into the room, leaves him standing in the hall. He feels better that he doesn't look bad enough for her to actually try to dissuade him from buying. He stares at the ridiculous mural along the length of the hall, so foreign to him compared to that of his own floor. The unfamiliarity reminds him of just how poor the execution of the art is—so unusual in Japan, where God really is in the details—ironic for a people that consider themselves ultimately A-religious. But what better god to worship? Maybe it's the owner's inside joke, since this *is* a rooming house primarily for *outside people*. But with some Japanese. Maybe a comment on what to expect from the mix.

And he laughs as he realizes that is more seconds of thought uninterrupted by the smoke than he's had in a long time—ironic that the giving in is so calming it almost negates the need for the drug itself. He wants to hold onto that thought, but she's back, holding out to him the tiny baggy he craves.

"Fust thing you dyu, yuu take a bleedin' showuh, fo the good of uzol, ol rite?"

"Ol rite."

And he does just that and he does feel better; nothing like washing away your yesterdays. He eyes the little baggy on the bed and wonders if it isn't that that has done the trick, the anticipation of relief bringing relief itself. He picks it up, and instantaneously feels scared. Truly scared. It's one thing to have to pound a few before a party to summon the will to go, but it's another entirely to have to smoke hard drugs in order to feel any kind of non-dread about any given minute. He distracts himself another moment by taking his insects and bringing them to the window, lifting the lid off, and dumping them all out. But it feels meaningless, like dumping insects out a window. He puts the box down and looks to the bed. Something in the marrow of his bones says get away from that bag, don't fall past the event horizon again, don't go lightly back into gluttony, back to addiction and self-absorption, back to doing nothing good, back to consuming ingesting excreting hurrying entropy along, taking in beauty and organization and leaving nothing behind but toxic sludge and useless excuses. Back to being a traitor to your kind. To yourself.

Just get away.
Now!

The bag drops as his fingers open just enough, as if on their own, an autonomic response to a searing he's too numb to feel. He turns and runs out of the room with the baggy left behind to sag on the bed, trying to put as much distance between himself and it while he still has the power to punch away the flurry of commands in his head. He has to run, run, run. He runs to the train station and the Eastbound rumbles in with the weight of a warship on rollers and the reassuring ability to take him far away. He beats himself onto it.

14th Floor

[on which everything can always be repaired]

"Please be careful. Doors opening. Floor fourteen."

Fucking hell.

14?

14 + *2* = 16

!

Two more floors!

Almost there.

…

…

…

"Yes. Like that."

…

…

Knife still there.

Box still there.

…

…

"This is it, my friends. Doors closing. Almost there. Fifteenth and penultimate floor next. We're running out of options."

Ready.

Totally.

Some nausea, some trembling.

T minus.

Jesus.

Yep, this is for real.

Real as it gets.

"Let me just say one last time, we hope you find everything you're looking for. You might not know it when you see it, and you might think you know it when you don't see it, but be diligent."

…

…

…

Wow, some clarity of mind!

He'd thought he was going to Kyoto for the idyllic Zen calm and grace, maybe sit and stare at Mishima's Golden Temple and instead of burning it down, meditate on how he could turn himself into something so perfect and beautiful, but then he'd pictured Ayumi's green-flecked crying face and wasn't sure he deserved anything good ever again. So he'd carried on all the way to Hiroshima, because that's what he's been doing to himself with the drugs—dropping nuclear bombs on his brain, razing everything built up over time and irradiating the rubble.

Now, after 24 hours mostly sleeping in his capsule, he feels an inch better physically but a mile worse mentally. He finds just enough energy and motivation to get out of bed and get some food and water and see some different walls. But in this city, where few of the walls are older than 70 years thanks to man's desire to demonstrate his ability to knock them down, he's overwhelmed by a depth of connection to a universal sadness that stirs up a splashing of acid in his soul that reaches to his eyeballs and stings, though no tears come. His emotions are stampeding bulls that he has neither the will nor the heart to try to control; if they trample him they trample him and so be it.

And so he goes to the heart of the matter, and in the Peace Museum, staring at the slab of concrete wall tracked with black rain stains, like mother earth's mascara-laden tears streaming down her cheek, while the babbling river of yellow-capped school kids eddies and flows around him, just the thought of how man could turn something as right as rain—even rain itself—to a wrong, leads him to weep uncontrollably, almost wail, this block of concrete a vision more powerful than any work of art ever created, by him or anyone else. He feels eyes on him and a great fear fills him. He doesn't know what exactly is alive within him, but he knows he has to get away from all these eyes attached to brains probably taking him for a 外人 overdoing a guilt about something he can never understand like they do. He drags himself through the soft darkness past the display boxes glowing warmly, the light so soothing and the contents so devastating. Here a child's tricycle that looks like, well, it survived a nuclear holocaust—and the card says it belonged to a child who died from his burns, and his father buried the thing with him till it was dug up 40 years later. Again, Ayumi's angelic face, one minute the essence of sweet reading words in an alien language, the next … And he couldn't even comfort her, console her or make amends, just run away to take care of himself. He imagines her body charred and blistered and monsterized like all these pictures of "survivors" on the walls that more than a few people are taking pictures of for some unimaginable reason.

Jesus, he needs *out* of this place.

What kind of fucking idiot comes somewhere like this in his state?

Blinded by the darkness he escapes the museum and puts one foot in front of the other and the other and the other, not caring what direction, only knowing the sun in his eyes is blinding and therefore helpful.

Two hours later he steps onto the famous Shrine Island of Miyajima. The emptiness of the ferry and the silent openness of the Seto Inland Sea have left him feeling lighter, vaguely in control again, and as he peruses the airy openness of shrines and temples at peace, he feels energized by them. Along with tufts of his hair, the ocean breeze lifts his spirits in what feels like the glory of first flight.

At Daishoin Temple he pays his entry fee to the smiling white- and orange-clad *Shingon* acolyte and walks up the empty boardwalk and into the lush verdure and gardens and ponds and peaked wooden roofs of the temple complex nestled into the crook where two arms of the holy Mount Misen meet. What's most striking is that there's no one to be seen; all he knows is crowds, everywhere. Even on the hiking trails in the mountains surrounding the Kanto plain, always a steady stream of people; even on back streets at five in the morning, someone, and the sense of someone on the other side of walls, humanity everywhere. Here, with no one around but every leaf of every tree dancing in the wind, water flowing through ponds and over stone outcroppings toward the sea, muscular carp wiggling in the depths and birds gliding through the heights, tiny flies flitting by and their wings buzzing the sunlight, it's the opposite of lifeless.

He removes his shoes and steps into the main temple and marvels at the precise workmanship of the wood and the faded paintings of times and places long gone. At the back corner is a set of stairs leading up, so up he goes, the cold wood creaking beneath his socks as he ascends the four red-carpeted flights. He steps into a single *tatami* room with sliding windows along three walls, all open to the views. The architecture is light as air, as if it's a building inside out, and it's how he feels in his head, gorgeous open emptiness. He looks out the window and sees the entire temple complex below, the valley spilling into the village and the sea holding it all in place. He looks at the sharply defined orange lines of the Shrine's famous "floating" *torii*, the gate through which supposed spirits are welcomed in. And, presumably, out? The tide in, it's standing in water now, the selfie-sticked tourists and sea-urchin hunters he'd seen earlier now disappeared, along with everyone else, as if the sea has erased them, perhaps to give him this solitude, this moment to notice the details, to not be distracted by the presence of others.

As he looks at the pristine view built by man to both accent and glorify nature, he's touched by authenticity and he realizes he does not actually want to see all of man disappear so that nature can be left to remain beautiful; what he wants is to see mankind become once again a part of nature's beauty. Even just *him*. He's filled with a hope he isn't sure he's ever felt before, a ray of sunlight reaching into the depths of his being, not angling away, only brightening.

The next morning he awakens in his capsule with his brain drenched in the wet paint of yet another hyper-vivid dream painting, his heart racing, and actually mouthing the words *where the fuck is land?*

He was in the sea, the middle of it, cold, sharks circling, and over there a beautiful yacht with gold fixtures and fur-lined window portals and railings, beautiful women in diamond bikinis and men in expensive suits calling to him to come aboard, laughing and holding out crystal goblets, being served by other people wearing rags and collars around their necks and giant diamonds shackled to their ankles, a vast table loaded with food, fruits, vegetables, and grilled human limbs, with a blackened human head as a centrepiece. And over there another yacht, the same beautiful people but of a different colour than the first, and over there another with the same minor variations; all he needed to do was swim over and reach for one of the outstretched hands. And he was exhausted, utterly spent, unable to tread water any longer, bleeding from a wound in his abdomen, the sharks getting closer and closer and the panic of being unable to think of a way to escape them, other than just inhaling the salt water and letting death take his life away before the sharks tore apart his body. Or letting one of the boats bring him aboard, of course. Absolute desperation for the sharks to just go away. How the fucking hell did he even get out here? He had resigned himself, fully and realistically and actually quite peacefully, to drowning, when he woke up.

"Fucking hell," he says to himself, holding his head, the meaning of the dream ridiculously obvious, even for one who believes dreams mean shit. But he's determined to control his mind again so he beats back the thoughts and picks up the comforting blanket from yesterday and finds that it works still. And he's hungry again and he laughs because all he needs is something to eat. And how easily procured is something to eat!

He sets out and the first place he comes across is a Yoshninoya but that's crap so he carries on a little further down the road and comes upon a *ramen* shop, a couple rungs above crap. As he eats he looks at the beer bottles in the fridge and they call to him and he thinks of having one but decides it's better not to play with fire. Then he thinks about it again;

it's not like he's some sad lifelong alcoholic fucking useless junky who can't be trusted to have one beer without falling back off the deep end! But still, proving to himself that he has control again is more important for this moment. He pays his bill and chats with the incessantly smiling woman who's shy but thrilled to talk to a foreigner in her own language. They discuss the city and she pretends to refuse to believe he's only lived here three years with such good Japanese, and she's all squinty eyes and nods to hear him say that he's never witnessed anything more beautiful in the world, nothing in the world more beautiful than this country and its people.

He walks aimlessly, through back streets, enjoying the decidedly hot weather, trying to just exist in the moment, like a good Buddha. He comes across a weather-worn neighbourhood shrine. Devoid of people, it seems to come from a time beyond or after, without. He sits on the platform of cracked planks surrounding it like a moat and meditates. Not very successfully, but he does sit still for 10 minutes. Thoughts buffet him, but they feel somewhat meaningful so he allows himself to dwell on some of them. Like the one about Sakura's samurai tattoo being so damn wrong on her. How she's only obeying the negative aspects of the concept. And her damn us-and-themness. How the world needs to escape that crap. *Goddamn,* when will it escape that crap? And *how?* So ironic, that being the name of her perfume.

Anger rises, pushing the good away, so he gets up and sets his body in motion and focuses on the one foot in front of the other, walking the barrel-earth. Though he feels weak and still somewhat nauseated, he keeps walking and ends up coming across a tattoo parlour, which seems serendipitous until he sees the sign that says it's closed. Strange, being as how it's 1:30 on a Tuesday. As he thinks about it the more convinced he becomes of the rightness of what he's thinking. He's never been one for tattoos, always sort of looked down on them, considering them a low form of art placed on the most valuable canvas possible, but he decides that in this battle this might be helpful, and tattoos were originally battle markings, weren't they? Decided, he takes another look at the nondescript building and thinks it shouldn't be a problem to find an open tattoo parlour on the main streets. But something about this one feels right, the fact that he just came upon it, as if *it* came to *him*—that's how he's meant to get a tattoo. He knocks on the door, worried about possibly disturbing someone's meditation, but deciding that if the person can be disturbed by him this way there's meaning in that.

And a man comes, looking nothing at all like you'd expect the owner of a tattoo parlour to look; in threadbare sweater and shorts and flip flops, not a drop of ink visible on his skin anywhere, you'd guess he's a businessman on Sunday. The eyes are wise, weary, but they brighten when they see him, as if he'd been expecting someone that he hadn't really thought would come.

"Yes?"

"Are you the distinguished owner of this fine art studio?" says Will, honestly full of reverence.

"Yes."

"I see you are closed, and I deeply regret disturbing you, but I am humbly hoping to receive a tattoo from you. A very simple one. And I hope you would be so kind to offer it to me outside of your regular hours, as I've no doubt your regular schedule is booked solid."

"If your need is so great, who would I be to turn you away?"

"You would be a man acting most within the bounds of decency and I assure you I would take no insult."

The man offers the door to him and steps aside, bowing, ushering him in.

Will follows him into a tiny studio, the room lit up by the sun pouring in the window. The studio's not at all what one would expect, either; there isn't a single sample of tattoo art on the wall, not a single pipe for sale in a glass case or a single scantily clad model on an eccentrically decorated wall. The floors are wide plank hardwood and the walls white plaster between deeply fissured wood beams, the ceiling dark wood as well. The only things on the walls are Zen paintings of rarefied beauty, the black and white in such perfectly decided contrast that it seems the argument for colour was lost hundreds of years ago. He's almost giddy with excitement over how this could not be more perfect.

"Would you like some tea?" says the man and Will can't refuse his offer. "Please, have a seat," says the man, at the counter, pouring hot water into a small handleless cup through a tea colander full of shredded green leaves. Will sits in the silky smooth wooden chair he has motioned toward. "Since you express such great need, I assume you know exactly what you want and do not need to see the sample folders?"

"No sir, it's just a few words. I understand if you are not able to do *Romaji* ..."

"Oh, I can do *Romaji*," he says.

"Fantastic," Will replies. "What I'd like is, on my inside left wrist, the English word 'Escape' in small but wide capital letters with three exclamation points after it, with the *kanji* characters for close and then open on either side of it. And on the front side of the same wrist, the *kanji* character for samurai."

The man, no older than 40, but with the confidence and assuredness of one who's lived lifetimes, comes to him and hands him the tea. "Those are most interesting symbols," he says. "There are a number of interpretations and characters for each of those concepts."

"Most certainly, sir. I know which ones I want, though."

The man does not look any more or less impressed that he did a moment ago. "Your Japanese is very good, and I'm sure you know what you're doing, but in this profession I believe part of my art is to ensure that my canvases know what they're committing to."

"That is most admirable and appreciated."

"So, may I ask one more question?"

"I would not dream of denying you."

"Samurai, well, we know that for Westerners it is a romantic image, and *cool* and *trendy*, but do you know that many Japanese believe this is shameful."

"Well, all art is open to interpretation."

The man laughs boisterously, the laugh of a Dalai Lama. He settles and says, "But, are you sure you wouldn't prefer a skull or an anchor."

"Those are most interesting symbols as well, no question. But in the West you don't get an anchor tattoo unless you have sailed across an ocean, so …"

The man nods his head knowingly and smiles.

He feels like he's passed a test and it feels damn good. He almost feels *respected.*

As the artist gets his equipment ready, Will thinks of how it seems that this was *meant* to be, that this is for a reason. He's always despised such notions, considering them weak and childish, logic-bending and ultimately disrespectful. But still.

He will make it so by his actions.

He will live up to this treatment. And this tattoo.

He will not disappoint.

He will never accept the hand extended over the handrail.

He will swim to land or die trying.

He *will never use again.*

15th Floor

[on which dreams delineate reality]

No one steps out at 15 but a man and a frail old lady are stepping in.

His final audience.

Captive.

A stinging in his eyes. A welling of emotion. A need for honesty and to pay recognition. No more appropriating.

"Next floor is sixteen. My word, let me tell you how many superb restaurants and places there are to take a relaxing break from your important shopping." Fuck. His voice is trembling.

Press 閉.

As he waits for the floor to press against them all, he thinks of their height, the debt owed to gravity, the danger they're all in.

The beautiful defiance.

The man has his left hand on the shoulder of what can only be his mother in front of him. Grey at the roots of her hair. He wants to hug her. He wants to hug him.

He wants to hug them all.

Invite them to share their deepest fears and worries.

Make them feel better.

But that won't help anyone.

And there is work to be done.

The blanket held and kept him warm the whole way home and he fell asleep wrapped in it. This morning, though, it's heavy, damp and musty and weighing him down; a beautiful young woman aged and desiccated overnight, like you slept your life away. He tries not to notice, wraps it around him again, and heads out for breakfast, forcing a smile the whole way as he walks the five minutes to the shopping street, dodging bodies and bicycles and billboards and every millisecond reminding himself why he's carrying this weight on his shoulders. And as he sits waiting for his set lunch of mackerel, rice and miso soup, the blanket starts to feel like lead, like they put on you when you get an x-ray at the dentist, but instead of the reassuring embrace of mother with nothing but the best intentions of comfort and place and protection, this is smothering him, gravity pulling harder and harder on it, trying to crush him under it. Why? What has gravity got against him? What the hell did he ever do to piss physics off?

His food arrives and he plays with it, no longer hungry, the way the meat separates so readily from the bone reminding him of how ultimately willing everything is to fall apart. The blackened eyes don't even stare at him accusingly, for they're not eyes anymore, just circles of carbon in a skull. Just atoms. Everything just atoms. Strings. The cells of this fish, of the fish he beheaded with Sakura, of Sakura, of cherry blossoms and roses and psychopaths, of Ayumi and the incinerated of Hiroshima, all of them just forever shape-shifting since the beginning of time, joining new parties, new constellations and systems and then leaving for other pastures.

The beginning of time. The beginning. A fresh start. No past to make up for. When every thing came into thingness. Versus non-thingness. The earliest universe, as much matter as now, but crammed into a space smaller than an atom. Near infinite density, near zero spatial extension, yet still the universe, just not mind-blowing in the dimensions we're used to it being mind-blowing in. Yet still mind-blowing! And composed of what? Why that infinitely dense something rather than the nothing around it? That old nugget.

He looks around him, shapes, colours, textures so familiar, and he again tries to think why all this instead of nothingness. Buddha inanely says it's nothing ultimately, all of it, but what the fuck does that *really* mean? Do you have to be Asian to really get it, because in the rub he sure as hell doesn't. There *is* something instead of nothing. A piece of lint, the Burj Khalifa. He *is*, as opposed to isn't. Don't ask what, or for what purpose, but definitely *is*. For now. Until his clock stops ticking. The same for all of us. ISIS killers and ISIS killed. Not is *is*, but is made *was*. You die and become one with timeless eternity and your meagre years of existence are put into perspective and suddenly you're all time and none of it, all at once. And laughing you'd say to yourself, if you had a self and a say, Jesus Christ we mean nothing!!

He looks at the old man in the corner, soon to die no doubt, that body coming to rest at last. But not at all, the atoms will become more active than they've been in a long time, dissipating, taking up residence in other systems. He thinks of dead bodies, thinks of the images of Michael Brown lying dead in the street, again *us* and *them*. No propaganda, just one sad arrangement of atoms versus every other. He couldn't stop looking at it. The trail of blood, the indignity, the collapse of the wave, the heaviness, the lumpiness. The *indignity*. The vicious and perversely insidious irreversibility. When a body's alive it seems so perfect, so well thought-out and assembled, so utilitarian. God is in the details and none have been overlooked with the human body. But dead? It seems so unwieldy, cumbersome, awkward. A cadaver epitomizes uselessness. No longer a miraculous feat of engineering, but a pile of soft stuff with some hard parts here and wet parts there—crusty parts here, smooth parts there. Here's a round shiny thing; looks like a marble wrapped in flesh-coloured wax.

And when this change of state is forced upon you or someone you love because of racism or greed or simple pleasure …

!

No question the high of Mount Misen's fucking over.

This is low again. But, a different low.

Just have to get through the days, know the brain will rebalance itself in time.

But lost in mechanism and engine and math, he's wrong, surely?

There's more to existence than that!

Is what he's always believed?

Art reveals it. A beauty and meaning deeper than just a pretty face.

He needs this now, deep infusion of meaning, of beauty, like a man in shark-infested waters needs a cage around him. So he gets on the train and at Tokyo Station transfers to the Yamanote and four stops later is exiting Ueno station and heading to the museum, on the grounds of which he sees posters announcing the final week of an Andy Warhol exhibit at the National Museum of Western Art. Andy Warhol. Of all possibilities. Yes, his themes were important, insightful and prescient, but. … He thinks of just going to the Tokyo National Museum, as he'd intended, but he can't resist, trying to believe again that maybe there's meaning in this too, that maybe the universe does have an answer for him and is trying to guide him to it, to dry land at last.

The place is packed. People wanting to see this plastic crap. *Japanese* 人々. Well, Japanese 人々, but also black 人々 and white 人々 and brown 人々 and plenty of white boy/Asian girl couples, the faces of whom he can't bear to even look into.

So packed. Is this it? Does this sum it up? They're just being gracious, encouraging in a wiser-than-thou kind of way? Patronizing? Using us for entertainment. They know, despite the company line, it's *us* that are shallow and *they* that are deep. We'll never be as good as them and they know it, and they know we think the opposite, and we don't know we're wrong and they do; they may have been beaten by a terrible weapon, but they've shown in the end who's better. And they use us, for our sense of romance and adventure and passion, our childish selfish individualism that results in pretty good entertainment and sex. Our attachment we can't let go of and they can go slumming in.

He comes to the car crash pieces and over the top of the black-haired heads he's pulled into the turquoise print. A fifties Ford or whatever is lying upside down after a crash, defying gravity and creating space for the people under it, as if sheltering them. Your eyes are immediately drawn to a woman's body, slightly awkwardly laid out but seemingly in one piece, no visible damage, but you know she's dead, something in the arrangement and stillness of her lower legs.

Something is unfixably broken in there. The black smudge that must be blood should help with understanding, but it seems so separate from her, attached rather than derived. Not even blood? Apart from her a man and a woman are lying on their stomachs, half out under the car, propped up on their elbows as if on a carpet watching TV. The man, he's looking to his side, seemingly at the dead girl, but not necessarily; half his face is blacked out by the black smudge as well. The other girl, the only eyes that can be looked into, don't show surprise, or fear, or sadness, or even emptiness; it's primordial, it's the clarity of no thought, only being. Where you would expect terror or amazement, there is only void. Is she in touch with the nothingness, with the no-meaning, with the quirk/quark state and the hardness of the pavement? Is she possibly dead too?

And, what you're left wondering ultimately about, as the two men in front of him are discussing: in the age before cell phones and pocket cameras, who on earth took the picture?

Escaping the mad crowd and putting Warhol behind him he walks through the main courtyard and decides there's nothing to do but go and see Julie. Reach for that hand outstretched over the railing. Really. What shit is he buying into with this fear? Does he not have control? Can he not choose his own terms? Right now *and* next week? Why is he so fearful of what *may* come? The future is unknown, always deliciously unknown. Every new day a chance to slay your demons, *or* make peace with them. There might not even *be* a future! If the ship's no good he can just jump overboard again. Maybe even commandeer a lifeboat, or at least a life preserver. But as he scans his surroundings, to the east he catches sight of Tokyo Skytree. Right there. A beacon? A gigantic buoy? He's been meaning to go see it. Maybe he can put off Julie just a little longer.

He heads for it, and along the way, to try to distract himself even more, gets a new iPhone and plays around with it for about 10 minutes, but it makes him think of calling Sakura and so he almost throws it away, but puts it in his pocket instead. He crosses the Sumida and walks along it partway, then through narrow residential streets of Shitamachi until half an hour later he's at the base of Skytree and he imagines what Sakura would have to say and he banishes her from his thoughts for the millionth time. He waits in line the 20 minutes for a ticket, then the 15 more minutes for the elevator, and then is moved with his group to a darkened entrance stall to await the arrival of the elevator. To his left is a female staff member, telling them the elevator will arrive shortly, and other facts in the meantime. She's gorgeous, of course, decked out in the stylishly baggy dress of battleship greyish blue and pale yellow, two of his favourite colours to paint with. The pattern is basically stretched triangles, alluding to the shape of the tower, he presumes, grey pointing down and yellow pointing up. And she smiles and smiles and her voice rolls and rises and descends enthusiastically as if what she's got to say is the most amazing thing she's ever heard and retold and retold and retold. He remembers Sakura asking him if this was his goal and he knows he could never rise this high. You have to be an insider. You have to know how to Japanese. Like this girl does. So perfect. So authentic. So seemingly of here and nowhere else, organic and native, not an ounce of awkwardness or absence to her. So cute and unforced. A flawless ballet dancer. Anger rises and he knows that if he were high the feelings resulting from his thoughts, no matter what they were, would be the opposite of what they are at this moment.

And if this girl loved him?

The elevator arrives and he steps in with everyone and the girl sees them in, says bye to them, and bows deeply as the doors close with her on the other side of them, leaving them to the cold machinery. Yet another driverless elevator in Japan. He wants to bow to the beautiful almost conductor who can never love him, but the door's already closed and he can only see himself in the mirror and so he closes his eyes and feels the floor elevating them all to lofty heights that they're all just going to have to come down from again in the end.

He walks around the viewing platform, swimming through the すごい, 素晴らしい, and 良いねs, and sees the sun's soon to set. He walks more, notes the map that shows the tower is taller than the CN. Good for it. Taller maybe, but the viewing platforms of each are the same height. Looking out on the concrete Kanto sea it feels a lot taller than the CN, but then he realizes it's because the CN has taller buildings surrounding it, and so its view is far more interesting in the angles and perspectives and architecture and movement. And the CN *rotates.* And the CN's certainly more beautiful. Maybe not the elevator attendants or their uniforms, but the structure itself. More graceful, organic; like this is a child's toy made of Popsicle sticks and toothpicks, origami. … It's light, though; more like a *sakura* petal, while the CN is heavy, like a rose? … And this is so rigid and youthful and new. Earthquake-proof and nimble. The concrete CN so … old. Old.

"Dear customers, let us take this opportunity now to tell you how much we love having you grace our floors. People who want nothing but to increase the beauty in this world and minimize the ugliness. And you're so good at it. So practical, so secular, and yet so intricate and divine in the way you do it. And yet so humble! Know we love you. And not just our Japanese customers, but our foreign ones as well. You're all so beautiful when you're beautiful. When you're beyond yourself."

Voice still trembling. Now his hands too. Writhing *hara*.

"And now, valued customers, be aware, doors will soon be opening at floor sixteen, the top, nothing more to offer. If you can't find what you're looking for here, may we suggest you head back down and look more closely. Because there's nothing more we can think of to offer you. The answer must lie below. Maybe we could all try a bit harder. Just know that we're here to serve you. Always. It's all for you. Please be well. If we should never meet again, just know I …"

Keep it together man!

Jesus Christ, *why* is he doing this to himself? What the fuck is this? Self hatred? Self-effacing violent attraction to the Other? Is this yellow fucking fever? Is this just overthinking everything? Is this *madness?* But if there's nothing, if nothing fucking matters, if we're just dust, bubbles in a bubble universe in a bubble universe, if that's the case, well ... he might as well go and buy some *shabu*. And the rightness of that thought, which comes so diplomatically, so logically, so soothingly motheringly, becomes unassailable. He *tried*, but reason must win out. And though he's not completely committed, his body obviously is, because it hurries him down to the road and his hand is up and he's in the back seat of the cab and the door is closing and sealing him away in another box, but it's not even close to sealing enough; he's still bleeding out. And then he's home and he's heading to Julie's door and he prays to God she's there and if she isn't would she be so mad if he jimmied her door and took her stuff? He'd pay her whatever she wanted. And then he's at her door and he forces himself to take a moment to reconsider and at least clean himself up a little but he's knocking on her door and she's there!

She comments on him looking healthier, heavier, and sells him three bags. He asks her if she'd like to have some with him, because who knows, maybe that would help, but she tells him she has plans, which probably means she doesn't herself use but she's not about to tell her customers that, not that any of them would give even a fraction of a shit, in fact they'd be happy in so far as that means she's reliable and less likely to die tonight and deprive them of their source. He takes it to his room and without a second thought smokes some and within 30 seconds he feels better than he's felt in days and he wonders why he doesn't just let his body do its own damn thing; who the fuck is he to think he knows more than it does, millennia of sexy progenitors who found a way to get laid while also surviving, all this wisdom he thinks it's wise to defy? His body fucking knows! And with that the Mount Misen business is officially dismissed like piss in a gilded urinal, a paranoid fucking delusion sliced ruthlessly in half like some idiot who pissed off the wrong samurai.

This is real and this is gorgeous.

If there is a god, he put this here and wired our brains this way so we could approach him.

God.

Kami.

神.

Such uninspiring *kanji.* Just some guy lost to the world, praying at an altar.

But, add a few dots and a line and you end with 禅. *Zen!*

He'll demonstrate *god* qualities. *And* Zen.

He'll become again a man of *action.*

動作.

He pulls out his paints and sees he has no clean canvases left, so he takes one of his portraits of Sakura, his favourite, and pulls the staples and flips the canvas around, then staples it back in place, whistling while he works. He takes a few more huffs and feels capable of anything, any fucking anything, and he doesn't think about what a year of living like this might mean because this is the only moment that exists, this here-and-now which needs to be seized and he damn well will! Just look at him go! He thinks and thinks and a million good ideas come to him and then he settles on the elevator girl. He looks up Skytree staff on Google Images hoping to find an image of her and he actually does. He decides she looks nothing like Sakura at all. And he sets to painting her. And he feels perfectly activated, in place, sealed into meaning, creating life before his eyes with his own hands, brain and heart and mind and *hara* all focused on this most important of tasks. And as he applies paint to the raw canvas he feels perfectly at one with everything, perfectly, essentially, not there. And he takes another huff to celebrate. He looks to ESCAPE!!! painted on his wall as if by some lunatic in a paranoid fit and he laughs. He takes a few more huffs and, to prove a point, one of magnitude, he gets down on the floor, forces his legs into a proper lotus sit, which kills his left ankle, puts his hands together in his lap, rights his back, levels his chin, and starts counting his breath. And for about nine seconds it feels incredibly important, like he's defeating something, or joining something worth joining, but before long he's barely able to get to three seconds before his mind's fucking with his count and asking him what on earth he's doing doing nothing instead of something.

But all this *is* something. In a mad world only the mad are considered sane. Either he is, or he isn't, but whichever it is he feels right and all you can do is go with that. This is as close to perfect as you can get in this desperately far-from-perfect world. You'd have to be insane to *not* use drugs. And he refocuses on the floor three feet in front of him, trains his gaze, focuses, stills, ceases, seizes.

One second.

One more second.

One more second.

One more second.

One mo—

He notices some paint spilled there.

One more sec—

And then he *really* notices the paint spilled there.

One—

His whole being shudders.

A collective molecular groan.

He vomited on a kid.

?

!

A *child. Kodomo*. 子供.

And then he ran away. To save himself. A little girl. A daughter. Someone's 少女. A little girl with a mother that looks upon her the way his mother looked upon him. Probably wanted to kill him. How would she look upon him at this moment? How would his mother look? How does he look? How would a brain scan look? A measurement of his morality?

What the fuck is wrong with you?

?

!

He goes back to his pipe, takes another head-clearing huff. Tries to just paint, watch what forms, but he sees it is not good. His hands are shaking, his precision is shot, his will to be precise is gone, his belief that it matters in the slightest shattered seemingly irrevocably. And then, yep, there it is, a fucking welling in the eyes and now a tear actually dripping onto the defiled and pointless canvas. "Fuck sakes," he says, taking a deep breath and wiping his eye with his forearm. "Get fucking real," he commands himself. "Sentimental fucking bullshit!" But the room's four walls are getting tighter, wanting to square him like a rusted-out relic in a junkyard car compactor, rid him of his emptiness, no fucking escape, despite the writing on the wall. Just another door leading to more of the same.

And loneliness isn't even the word for it.

Aloneness gets closer, but ultimately misses the point. That being alone is fine, as long as you like yourself. As long as you're trapped in the mind of someone who has something, any fucking thing to offer this world. He used to be a man of action, he went to fucking jail for his principles! But that him is dead. This is him. *This*. This fucking useless addict who ran from the war and whose heart's racing and whose hands're shaking and whose brain's rudder's been ripped off in the violent surf where the gale winds of drug-state meet the cruelly bull-headed and boulder-strewn shores of reality.

"Whoa," he says and gets up. "Whoa fucking *whoa*." But this does nothing and he seriously considers calling an ambulance, asking to be locked away, but there's no fucking *away*. Bubbles. He's locked up wherever he is. But what's the point anyway? What's he so fucking scared of? So he dies. So he dies, he blinks out, becomes one with the atoms, timeless, of all time, outside of time, outside of self, outside of sides. Finally fucking nothing. Sounds great!

He focuses on his heart racing, dares it to go faster, and faster yet, but it doesn't. "That's fucking right," he says, grabbing his pipe and taking another hit, and another. Then he takes his knife and slits the canvas down the middle. He sits on his bed, flicks the TV on, BBC, lets go of the wheel and throws himself headlong at the headland of the real world's heady realities. Either it'll kill him or it'll make him stronger, and he's fine with either, because the status quo is now officially fucking untenable.

He smokes more and is able to keep his hull intact second by second by reminding himself he's lucky compared to the majority of people in the world, the endless march of sad souls through the 24-hour news cycle in constant need of replenishment and revelling in these times of plenty. Then, while watching a report on the child soldiers of Boko Haram, either executed for weakness or promoted for savage depravity, it hits him, the real storm after the squall that's already scared the living shit out of you, a violent rip through every delusion and sugar coating and rose-coloured lens he's ever used to strengthen his hull, the acid ugliness of his own existence, the hypocrisy of talk, of all talk and no action, of false, bleeding-gums compassion. Of taking the pain of others and raping it.

His heart's racing again, his mind out of control, his limbic system gone machine-gun-rampage-through-a-mall mad, his monkey brain saying once and for all enough's e-fucking-nough!

He looks to the Morrisseau on the wall, desperate for help, but it gives him the coldest shoulder ever thown.

Right this moment

Aboriginal girls lie face down and dead and rotting while the state focuses on tossing their brothers and parents in jail for drinking in public

A mother watches her daughter die of a disease that money could beat

A cow tries to move an inch to its left and can't and finds the same situation on its right

Someone beats back insanity while working the fourteenth hour in a row performing a particular hand motion that affixes one mechanism to another

Someone awaits the executioner's call

A dolphin/monkey/fish/elephant/person screams as its family is coldly slaughtered

Someone's 少女 restrains her gag reflex while some old man's erection pounds the back of her throat uncaring whether or not she chokes to death on his cock or his semen

Someone profits off all this

Jesus Christ

I profit off all this?

STOP!
STOP!
STOP!
STOP!
STOP!
STOP!
FUCKING **STOP!**

No.
It won't just because you want it to.
Sorry, but why do you reckon you deserve to get what you want?
Every bounce of an atom is political, and you elected to forget.

There is redemption. You're creative, you know, you know what to do. Be thankful for that.

And then, this madness that is terror galvanizes and clarifies and at last becalms. It's the giving-in to blood lust, the welding-shut of the pain gates, the separation of mind and body, the high of honour and the relief of no-tomorrow that matters. If you can't beat the sharks and hypocrisy, the last thing you do is *join* them. This is the kind of thing you go down fighting. There is no surrender to this. The best time to plant a tree was 20 years ago—the next best time is now. Surrender to this and God won't cry when you're tied by your ankles and hung upside down over a flame and burned to death head first. As has been done time and again throughout human—*your*—history. Unimaginable to you, but someone in their now suffered that. The curtains opened, and there they were, suffering that shit. And that. And that. And here they *are* this moment!

This is the kind of thing you go down fighting!
You take them down with you!
You never give in to it!
!

You pull out the biggest canvas you've been given in this life and you paint your fucking heart out.

16th Floor

[on which what goes up, comes down, one way or another]

Trailing the last customer out, box in both trembling hands, he wants to look back, see what happens to his elevator, but he doesn't, because he's actually a samurai now—and he knows the doors will simply close on their own and someone will press a button and the elevator will descend and spill its guts and no one will notice his absence. He walks past all the restaurants and out the doors onto the rooftop patio, which is crowded due to the warm cool of the gloaming. Past the seating area he winds his way through the ducts and vents and outlets and finds his spot looking out over the city facing west, the sea of structures of and for the people teeming within and about them, the JR train lines snaking their way through it all, what seems to cleave and separate actually bringing together and unifying, and all come neatly together below, leading in and out of 新宿 station, arteries and veins pushing out and pulling in both waste and sustenance to and from the body. And above all this the sun is making its way down and out now, seemingly sad for the lack of clouds, a whole pallet of paints it wants to use but no canvas to express itself upon. Like him in a sea of Japanese people. Like him in a sea of *people*. He wants to laugh at that—because what the hell else are you going to do with such a cheesy damn thought—but he doesn't. He sets the box down and takes the notepad and pen from his pocket and puts them down on top of it, then pulls the knife from the small of his back and rests it on the notepad. If he thought he could survive it he'd take an extra day and go and spend whatever it takes to get a proper knife, one from some renowned Japanese blade shop, some place making impossibly perfect points for hundreds of years. But this blade, dull as it may be in comparison to a proper *tanto*, will make as fine a point as any could.

And then he notices the damn thing would have easily fit in the box; why did he feel he needed to have it crammed into his belt at the small of his back all day?

Did he want to get caught?
Was he hoping for violence?
Does he have the slightest clue what he's doing?
Does he even fucking*Pound!*
Isn't it true that*Pound!*
Pound!
Pound!

He sits down in front of the box and opens it and pulls out the tripod, attaches his iPhone to it, then logs in to the Youtube account he created this morning and posted to his Facebook account, which he hasn't used in 10 months but is soon to become a lot more visit-worthy. Allowing not a thought of hesitation, of going back on this, he starts the streaming and sets the phone up in front of him so it's got his full form, and the only way to do that is to have the 生 character of the store's name over his left shoulder, Ikiruji (which means time to live (and *ikiru* is the title of an old Kurusawa film (the theme of which sure fits this!))). People will search for meanings of having this in the shot, but none of them will come up with the real explanation—nothing! That it just happened to be behind him. He looks up and sees there's a daylight moon, almost full. Should he count the meanings? What's the point? The hundred ideas he'd come up with would all just be yes-men of his own making. But one thing's for sure—the arena's full and he better not fail to perform.

Fuck he could do with a huff. One last one.

He looks to Tokyo, timeless and remade again and again, glorious and historical, spread out before him. Sakura out there somewhere. *Sakura.* He looks at his tattoo. Of *course* he was only a temporary construct for her—she's an intelligent woman of means with an eye on a fulfilling career. Women like that here don't get married anymore, especially not to foreigners. He's supposedly so deep and so worldly and knowledgeable about Japan—surely she was within her rights to expect him to know and understand that! He's a goddamned idiot, a hopeless idiotic Western romantic with the wit of a dim solipsist.

But, to be fair to himself—if not yourself, who?—what about Nitobe? She *meant* that!

But still, she's 桜, she's Japanese, she's loyal to her family and to herself, committed to action, to control. And here *he* is now, committed once again to the same thing.

Yes, here you are, aren't you? A junky with no better plan than to run away from it all and paint it as some grand Mishima-esque gesture—a gesture a wiser Mishima would surely take back if he could. And he wrote The Sea of Fertility*! What the hell have you achieved in this life? Just what exac*Pound! Pound! PoundfuckingPound!

He shuts his mind up, amazed once again at just how traitorous, how callously cruel the brain can be. He opens his notebook, puts the pen to the paper, but can't commit. A deluge of thoughts, but none worthy of being set down in ink, none worthy of soiling this perfect white page. Yet the paper is sucking out the ink, desperate for it. A black splotch forming, black invading the white. He stares hard at it, unblinking, his eyes drying out, starting to sting, tearing up a bit, but it's not from emotion, just necessity. He closes his eyes and tears out the page, crumples it up and throws it overboard.

Why do you have to do this? *Why don't you just paint, focus on the beauty, the miracle of simple existence? Add to it every day?*

Fucking hell! Give me a break, will you? Who the fuck can do that these days, slayed by the ever-present and accessible reality of 7 billion? How can there be any happy poets but the naïve? How can you tread lightly through life knowing what ground props you up? How can anyone focus only on the beauty? How deep inside your bubble must you be? This world will produce no more Whitmans!

The camera is catching all of this. It's already been uploaded. It's out there. He's on stage here! Better get a lot more samurai about this or just give up on the whole thing right now—what fucking direction are your shoes pointing!

He takes the Morrisseau out of the box and holds it up to the phone, then places it in his lap. Then he takes out the four cans of the most expensive lighter fluid he could find.

He looks to the camera, says, "I was going to do this in the elevator, that box that I've been steering but going nowhere in for so long, all the while helping people spread their wealth, ease a need for now and hopefully a little bit of later, but I don't want to hurt anyone. This is the opposite of that. If you have to hurt someone to prove a point, make it yourself that you hurt. …" He wishes he could press pause on this, but this isn't a movie by Kurusawa or anyone else; this is reality, a one-act play with no safety net.

He takes the knife in his left hand, turns it around to face away from who you think the enemy is when you don't know better, then he lifts his shirt and tries it out, pressing the tip into his belly below his navel, his *hara*, hard, harder, till it feels like it might break skin, and it hurts, but that is good and isn't going to stop him. *Hara,* 腹, where your existence is centred according to Zen and the most recent findings of intestinal microbiology—not your heart or your head, but your gut; the *kanji* which also can mean mind and courage.

Courage.

He will plunge this knife into his gut and slice from left to right, then spark the lighter and set himself on fire. All he has to do is sit still. Courageous people have sat like this and held a knife to their gut like this and plunged it in and cut before and thus it has been proven doable by the worthy. Properly performed, once the guts have been spilled, an honoured second does you the favour of cutting your head off for you, as prolonged dying by gut-spill is considered cruel and unusual punishment. But he has no second. And, more camera-friendly—and a nod to Sakura's idea of burning down the mall—is self-immolation. No one has ever combined these two acts, so this is Art that breaks new ground. Maybe the most painful suicide ever attempted, but for *Art.* Because art's easy but Art's *hard.* Because in times like these the only way to command air time is bigger and larger. Just sit still.

Or, is it all, still, even here, up here, now, for all the world to see, this, *still* just about ego?

God he wants a huff!

But how much did you smoke just hours ago? You're still high! Look what you're doing! You're nuts! And not the sane-in-a-mad-world kind of nuts, just nuts! Plain old nuts. If you're going to do this, fine, but do it with a clear mind—know *what you're bloody doing! You're no different than any other nut doing crazy things while high on power or lust or sadness or rage or religious delu*Pound!

He takes hold of the Morrisseau and holds it up to the phone. "Communalism versus individualism; it's only aboriginal thought that has solved this problem with any dignity. Like the acceptance that *you* are no more worthy than anyone else, but realizing this also means that no one else has the right to step on *you*. And they sussed it thousands of years ago, by being in tune with the rhythms of nature, by embracing powerful humility and wisdom. But the exploiters, they took the fool's gold and discarded the diamonds of wisdom."

That came out well enough. He wants to say more but he might ruin it. He looks to his notepad. He needs to write his death poem for Christ's sake. He looks out again. The Japanese sun has now set and the sky at the horizon is actually orange; the sun's made a canvas out of the nothingness after all. Fuji's fuzzily defined in black against the colour, so judicious and magisterial, so stately, so above it all—yet somehow still seeming apart, watching and caring? Like the matriarch watching the children play, enjoying but ever watchful and alert.

… Isn't that the opposite of this samurai silliness? Aren't most 日本人 now ashamed of all that, all that focus on honour and servitude which led to suicide bombers, which led to the cruelty of the war, justified by the idea that if your enemy surrenders they've given up their honour and are therefore no longer worthy of human consideration? Never mind the idea that hope and forgiveness and non-violence might offer more? Many don't even want to fly the rising sun flag anymore. But there are so many sides to such stories and symbols, infinite takes—the creative will see endless possibilities. Yet wasn't his Sakura experience a failure of such creativity? Didn't he judge and condemn her with only the first bit of understanding about her? What about the second bit, the third? Was that what she was saying with her *bushido* words to him? And whatever she meant, did he fight for her? Did he argue the point? Did he attempt to learn? Regardless of doctrine and culture and excuse, it's all just a failure of intellect, of creativity.

Fucking bubbles.

And that's as much bullshit as anything else.

He picks up a can of lighter fluid, opens it, and says, "So, I'm sorry to destroy it, but the point must be made. Most will lament the loss of this Morrisseau more than they'll lament the loss of me, and what does that say about us? Believe me, I believe in art, but to say that colour on canvass is more important than life, well, isn't that truly insane? Whether mine or hers or his or yours, how can a *human life* be of less value that an inanimate object? Time to go back to moral philosophy 101, I think, *world*! And how on earth can we think things as trite as money or power or comfort or power are? I'm a white man and I'm going to destroy a Morrisseau? I should *not have this power in the first place.* This world is organized such that I have the power to *own,* to destroy it. And people in this world also have the power to effectively *own* people, and destroy them."

He's feeling it; *nothing* enrages him more than thinking about the wrongness of the math the world has bought. He sprays the lighter fluid into a moat around him. He takes the second, trembling a bit now, and deepens the moat while also drenching his feet and legs and the painting. The third bottle he pours all over his upper body and shoulders, leaving only his head clear. His nose is nuclear-attacked by the very opposite of ESCAPE. He imagines the wispy column of smoke he'll amount to above Shinjuku, probably caught by a camera or three somewhere, impossibly thin.

How on earth did he get from there to here?

From a laughing cheering child to …

He imagines the billions of people throughout history who, on their deathbeds, thought that exact thing. He wonders if answers ever came to them.

He reaches for the knife, wishes he'd choreographed this more closely. Slice the Morrisseau, then slice his stomach, then light himself? Or, slice himself, then the painting, then light himself? Or, surely more resonant for the viewers, slice himself, then light himself, then, while on fire samurai slice the painting. Or …

He hears Tom, *actually* Aboriginal: if you're so damn willing to die honourably, why not *live* honourably? Sacrifice life, fine, but don't die! Use life to help!

And slice the Morrisseau? Are you fucking mad? Fucking help *is what you need!*

"I should have no right to own this," he says to the only ear that's bent to him. "True human freedom is the highest art. There has to be a minimum standard to human life, of human artefact, of human essence, that is preserved and sustained in every instance, regardless of circumstance, just for the health and wellness of our kind and all that is beautiful. Freedom is dying. The earth we know and love is dying. We must get active. We must act. In 25 years when your children ask you what you did once it became so obvious what the future was going to be like, what will you tell them?"

And you know you'll just be laughed at. Make the gaijin *newspapers. An embarrassment? Like your beloved Mishima became for most?*

He rubs his tattoo on his wrist, runs the blade across it. ESCAPE!!! Open. Samurai.

But samurai only did it when they had failed their master; are you not your own master? True, you've failed yourself miserably, but your master's not dead. Unless you *kill him! This is logically unsound—until you're dead you still have a chance to act. Amends can,* must, *be made! Who* is *your master? Earth. Mother earth. Mother of all; Japanese, Canadian, Russian, Chinese, American, just kids with their own bedrooms.*

He almost laughs at himself just to prove he still can. Then he remembers that he's on camera, where laughter at this time will be construed as insanity. And there *are* some things in life that are no laughing matter. That are just *not* funny. Life is not solely about entertainment. Some Art's *hard*.

He *has* let his mother earth down, he *has* failed her, and by *bushido* logic he *must* do this to regain his honour. *Better to die on your feet than have your honour broken. It's better to die a piece of jade.* … But since when was he so ideological? Doesn't he *hate* that kind of shit? And what kind of a mother would want that? Doesn't mother earth just want to see him get healthy so he can work again to stop the hurt being done to her right this moment? And live a full life? What good does he do dead? And doesn't he believe *all* violence is wrong? When he sees an execution of any kind, the complete and total theft of freedom, doesn't he weep and cry out in universal sadness for such soul-destroying ugliness? If we're all truly equal, should we not hold the same standard for ourselves as for others?

All this … just cowardice.

Selfishness.

He looks out over the city, tries to tap into the hope of 弥山.

Is he just afraid of the burn?

All those others who went before him, in this very moment, *they* dropped the match. There may not be someone somewhere else doing this *now*, but all those before him were in their own now, and they did it. And only the cowards and the exploiters and the idiots dismiss it as madness. They did it. It was real. It was as real to them as a novel set in the prairies with a tough heroine with bad skin who manages to realize she's as deserving as anyone and manages to win a grudging peace in life that's all the more rewarding for how unglamorous it all is?

He looks to his phone. This is all out there now. Everything since he started recording, watched this moment or later by anyone who knows him or wants to know this slice of him. There is no going back. If he gives up on this now, he'll be a world-wide joke. Probably even make the CBC. CNN sidebar maybe even. Jimmy fucking Kimmell?

Yes, yes, thank you so much, ladies and gentlemen. Thank you. Good evening, thanks, stop … thanks so much. … So, did you folks hear about the white guy who was going to burn himself to death atop a Tokyo department store? (INSERT PUNCHLINE HERE).

He presses the knife point deeper into his flesh.

The toxic smell is making him nauseous. Or it's the body wanting the *shabu*.

Cold sweat.

As he trembles and sweats and fights to make sure his guts come out by hand rather then mouth, he feels the eyes on him, and he suddenly realizes it's already done.

He's ruined it completely.

The not-doing is now harder than the doing.

If he walks away from this, for the rest of his life he'll be the guy that did that. This colossally embarrassing failure.

And *now*, if he goes through with it, it'll be just to avoid *that*?!

!

The whole soul and spirit of the Art is destroyed, and he truly is just a broken man committing suicide to escape a life that's too hard to live.

In a way that's heart-stoppingly devastating he remembers again the power of ideas, of art; now that he has thought this, there is no going back, the act and the outcome have fundamentally changed, a switch has been pulled, a phase change, the collapse of a probability wave. Every act of destruction …

And now he's truly trapped between floors.

*Now you've got it, you idiot! Get up! Do some real work out there in the real world! Who are you helping by leaving it to others to do the grunt work? If you can bear the pain of a knife in your belly, of sitting in fire and breathing in flames while your eyeballs boil, of taking a Morrisseau with you!, then you can bear*Pound! *the pain of doing some real work to make the world a better place for actual* *living breathing people, the trees that make up the forest you're so*Pound! *obsessed with. As much fury as you feel for any*Pound! *executioner, you should feel that for the part of yourself that has you here ready to go*Pound! *through*Pound! *with this*Pound! *If this* is *your self, you need to remake yourself, the* hard *way, not through violence and easy escape—rewrite the book!* Laugh at yourself! *Would anyone who can truly do that ever take the life of someone else?*

Do you even realize your mother is most likely Pound! Pound! Pound! *watching you this very moment?*

He looks to the camera, feels his mother's eyes on him, the horror she must be feeling. The inexpressible terror. The most pain a person can feel. Pain he can't even imagine.

!?

!?!?

!?!?!?

!?!?!?!?

!?!?!?!?!?

He snatches at the phone and holds the power button, choking it to death, then puts his hands to his temples and squeezes and groans deeper and deeper until it's hurting his throat and straining his vocal chords and vibrating through his entire essence and shaking the walls of his being, desperate for 開. The need for the drug calls to him and he throws wild punches at it, but it's too fast and he strikes only air. He quiets himself and lowers his hands. Looks out over the city, the millions of lives being lived, the millions of paths taken and not taken every single moment.

It's either move now or move never.

He gets to his feet, his legs stiff and sore. He expels a deep breath long and slow. He looks at the painting, seemingly impervious to the lighter fluid. He drops his heavy jacket from his shoulders and would drop the rest of his uniform from his body if it wouldn't affect his escape. But his trousers are pungent with lighter fluid as well, so he takes them off, figuring with his shirt untucked his longish black boxers can pass for shorts. And they'll never call a white person on it. Trains are rolling this way and the other down below and the city lights are waking up for another night of whatever it happens to bring. He takes the painting in hand and heads back into the mall, making his way to the stairs, opening the door and entering the stairwell and heading back down to earth, trying not to notice anything and trying not to think but unable to as ever, like trying to get the earth to stop rotating.

That elevator ride was supposed to be his last.

He was meant to never come down again.

Yet here he is.

He carries on down the echoing empty stairwell, carries on down, passing through floor after floor, each of this building's 16-actually-15-in-an-attempt-to-trick-death floors that he knows like the back of his hand but in name only—he knows what's supposedly on offer on each, but he's never actually walked through and seen for himself.

Just in his box. His bubble.

Rising and falling and giving direction but never taking it.

Ground Floor

[on which birds always signify land]

And like that he's standing on ground he never expected to see again, ground that appears solid but is far from it; below him are layers of people with things to do and choices to make, trains passing, chemicals and power and waste being moved, earth, rock, water, just ultimately a shallow layer of that, perhaps this moment readying to shift under his feet in the big one that'll bring the very building he was set to die on top of crashing down on top of him, and if that were to happen there'd be no way he wouldn't die with a smile on his face. And deeper still the mantle, molten, and then the solid core of iron—feels good to have something ultimately solid at the core of all this, but even that is shallow comfort, for when you compare the density of iron to the density of the early universe, well, it's essentially nothing. We're all so close to nothing, but *my*, the madness we mine from that! *Because* of that?

Just exactly *what* are we standing up for?

About where he's going he hasn't the first clue other than that he doesn't know, but that in itself is a clue. So he puts one foot in front of the other and joins the flow of people, people who look like they know where they're going and maybe they do. Something comforting in that. He can flow with this river of Friday-night people. But it's not like that, really, he still has to paddle. It takes effort. *Want to make God laugh?* he remembers Tom telling him. *Tell him your plans.* And as he passes by bar after *conbini* after *conbini* after bar, he wants to go and have some beer to celebrate, and that thought of course makes him think of *shabu*, which makes him shudder; he's not that old a dog, but he despairs for ever teaching himself new tricks.

So he just walks, past Shinjuku *gyoen*, which he considers going into, but it reminds him too much of Sakura and he's not exactly in the mood to rub his nose in that. He carries on and soon it's clear by the increasing volume of super *kawaii* girls that he's coming up on Harajuku. These ridiculous girls, seeming to *want* to look like they should be in plastic boxes on a shelf and sold and bought for a price. He's always thought fashion to be the lowest form of art—again, his PhD in judging—but now he wonders. You can read a lot of negative into all this, but these girls are *following* their passion. While he runs from his. He told himself he was packing it away, putting it aside until he honed his mind into a tool capable of handling the calibre of passion he was feeding it, but that's bullshit.

He thinks of everyone he's going to have to answer to.

What has he done?

He's starting to tremble again. Anxiety growing. Cramps and nausea. The *shabu*. He takes a deep breath and thinks of going to have a drink at least. Fear rises. More. Has he broken his brain? Ruined it for good? Turned it into a thing incapable of feeling pleasure? Is he destined to walk through life with a dour face and nothing to offer but snide cynical comments, like walking through a park with a needle in hand popping children's balloons?

... *Children*'s balloons.

... Ayumi.

Okay, is *this* what he came down from the damn roof for?

Maybe he needs to make a deal with himself—one more week. *One more week* of using, just for energy, to think, to come up with a proper plan. He needs his drug brain, because this brain can't do it. Once it has a plan, this brain will know what to do with it, but it needs the plan! Sometimes fire is used to fight fire. He will go to Julie and get a week's worth and promise himself seven days to come up with a plan for his life. He's certainly not going to come up with anything beautiful while trapped in this mind depleted of positivity, a fridge with nothing in it but empty ice trays and a burnt-out light bulb.

Meiji Shrine across the road.

Something deep tells him to go to it. Just keep walking a bit longer; go to Julie's, fine, but not this moment, not *this* one.

So he crosses the pedestrian bridge, tries to enjoy all the street performers and hawkers of jewellery and the doll girls, many of whom look at him but he's not sure whether it's because they like his *outside person* looks, or because he's wearing what on close look are obviously boxer shorts, or because he looks just as lost as he feels. He walks, hoping if he ignores the anxiety and nausea they'll just go away, fearing he's in for another hell train ride home. But he doesn't have to go home, he doesn't need Julie. He doesn't need her stuff; he can just walk into any bar and make a bunch of new Japanese friends and within 30 minutes have anything he needs. So he uses this thought to allow him to keep walking deeper into the park, a ground war, each footstep land brought under his command, though the fear is that he'll have to retreat. Up ahead the beautiful *torii* gate; can he make it to it? He'll just have to come back.

This shrine was destroyed, like most everything else in Tokyo, by the allied blitzkrieg. But he doesn't know specifically if the gate was. Could it have lived through that?

Despite his interest in the philosophical and practical side of Zen, it's always been Shinto shrines that he's most loved. In temples it's hard to avoid thinking about the religious elements, but in shrines, things feel humble, of nature, of an essence it's easy to imagine yourself part of. Because it's about the god in everything, Mother Nature as god. But, like Zen and any other system of beliefs, it needs to be tempered with a scientific agnosticism, or else you end up with foolish ideology and extremism—like the idea that the emperor of Japan was a living god (which is true, but only insofar as every living thing should be revered in the same way). But, throw that aside and you've got something very much in line with Aboriginal beliefs, with nature as god rather than God as god, and all the implications for man's idea of himself that result from that. It's the only creation philosophy that he has ever basically been able to find nothing morally *or* logically to fault. And yet look what has happened to this beautiful culture in Canada. Such a tragic irony. Why he wanted to burn the damn Morrisseau in his hands. The Morrisseau he has no right at all to impose his will upon, to kill. He can't believe he almost did it. Destroying it to prove he *should* have no power over it would have been a colossally tragic blunder; he'll paint his own paintings and destroy them if he thinks there's something to be gained by it.

Hey! That was good! That was a whole bunch of thought unrelated to fucking *shabu*! Or Sakura! Is it possible his brain's coming up with some good ideas in this state? Clearly this is a passion of his. Maybe he should study this shit or something. Would have the added bonus of giving his dad another fucking heart attack! Studying humanities!

He laughs and it feels good, but it jerks loose the trembling and the shakiness, the anxiousness, the blackness.

He looks to the gate again.

Torii.

鳥居.

Bird perch.

To this day they don't know whether it's a purely Japanese creation, or a foreign import. Yet it's accepted fully and completely, a fundamental element of Japanese identity. There's a relationship between birds and death in Japanese culture, but he's not sure of the details. Death; if he'd followed through he'd be there now. The great mystery revealed. Yet no revelation where there is no consciousness. We don't experience death, only dying. And what he's got coming round the bend is going to be way worse than being dead.

But that can all be analyzed later, his body says, because the nausea's knocking and if he doesn't get a huff in him soon he and everyone around him is in for trouble.

One last look at the firmly graceful 鳥居. Walk through that fucker dirty and come out pure. A car wash for the soul. Fast and efficient. Every step we take we choose purity or dirt. These gates are everywhere, unavoidable, in fact. The person is political. Every breath we take, *two roads diverged in a yellow wood.* He *has* travelled both.

A young woman is approaching the gate from the other side, a baby in some sort of baby backpack system at her chest and staring out ahead, pudgy arms out and grasping at the air.

He pictures her breastfeeding.

Such purity.

If she would do that now for him, would he be cured?

The pure essence of life.

Mother.

Haha.

母. Which, no two ways about it, is a depiction of breasts. Even in Spanish, *mama* literally means breasts. Mammary glands. A symbol not of humanity, but of *life,* of creation, of nurturance and of love. Sex, regardless of culture or affiliation, is at root about sustenance, about sustaining the species, nothing lascivious about it. A man grasping at breasts is re-enacting the most basic condition of the preservation of life, while *creating* it. He wonders what the *kanji* for sex is and can't believe he's never learned it. But he knows the *kanji* for *suki,* which means *like*: 好. Which is what? A woman and a child together. *Like*, the ultimate word for approval, particularly in today's Facebook world, is woman and child. It's all sex, it's all procreation, it's all breasts and food, and it's all so natural and right. And about children. And parents. And protecting them from puking junky teachers and a million billion lesser and worse catastrophes. Nurturing them, the most complex work of art man can create, and all part of a grand masterwork … An innocence that need not be lost.

He laughs, but it's gone even faster this time with a hard smack in the face; the crystal meth, the darkness and the false god and unloving mother making demands with increasing desperation.

He looks to the woman again, imagines her stopping, offering a lactating breast to her child. He wants to paint this. He's never wanted to paint anything more. He wants that sense of place and protection. He wants that smile. He wants that reassurance that there is an edge to this sea, a beach to finally roll up on, and at long last, rest.

"Hello? … *Hello*? …Who is this?"

"… It's me."

"Will?"

"… Yep."

"*Will!* Are you still in Tokyo? Are you *ok*?"

She *wasn't* watching it live. Thank God. "Suppose I could be better."

開

Acknowledgements

Thanks to Luciano Iacobelli and Allan Briesmaster for their hard work making this book better—and getting it into your hands.

Thanks to Susan, Nino, Pauline, Kathy, and James.

Thanks to my partner Aiden, the most beautiful thing in my life.

Thanks to Japan and its ways and people. Miyako Ide and Shizuyo Kaneko especially.

And my sincerest thanks to you, reader. I hope it was time well spent!

Other Recent Quattro Fiction

Loopholes by Showey Yazdanian
The Escape Artist by Anita Kushwaha
Too Much on the Inside by Danila Botha
The Duck Lake Chronicles by John C. Goodman
An Imperfect Man by John Calabro
JAZZ by Elizabeth Copeland
The Green Hotel by Jesse Gilmour
Down the Street by Cassandra Cronenberg
Costume & Bone by Lucinda Johnston
The Girl Before, the Girl After by Louis-Philippe Hèbert
Rough Paradise by Alec Butler
Look at Me by Robert Shoub
Dempsey's Lodge by Eric Wright
Inheritance by Kirsten Gundlack
Oatcakes and Courage by Joyce Grant-Smith
Terminal Grill by Rosemary Aubert
World of Glass by Jocelyne Dubois
The Sandbar by Jean-Paul Daoust
Texas by Claudio Gaudio
Abundance of the Infinite by Christopher Canniff
The Proxy Bride by Terri Favro
Tea with the Tiger by Nathan Unsworth
A Certain Grace by Binnie Brennan
Life Without by Ken Klonsky
Romancing the Buzzard by Leah Murray
The Lebanese Dishwasher by Sonia Saikaley
Against God by Patrick Senécal
The Ballad of Martin B. by Michael Mirolla
Mahler's Lament by Deborah Kirshner
Surrender by Peter Learn
Constance, Across by Richard Cumyn
In the Mind's Eye by Barbara Ponomareff
The Panic Button by Koom Kankesan